Rust Belt Redemption

NFB
Buffalo, New York

Printed in the United States of America

Coleman, David

Rust Belt Redemption/Coleman- 1st Edition

ISBN: 978-0615788135

1. Rust Belt Redemption . 2. Coleman. 3. Crime Fiction. 4. Detective Fiction

Cover photograph is of Central Terminal loacted in Buffalo, New York

No Frills Buffalo Press
119 Dorchester Buffalo, New York 14213
For More Information Visit Nofrillsbuffalo.com

More Tom Donovan Books

Shadow Boxing

Souvenir

For my mother and father for laying the foundation and my wife and daughters for making a home.

Rust Belt Redemption

By David C. Coleman

Chapter 1

Tom Donovan pushed his way through the outer office door.

"Tom, there you are," Grace said as she looked up from her desk just outside her husband's office. "Cal and Mr. Winters are inside. They want to see you."

Tom knocked and pushed the door open and was immediately hit by the smell of cigar smoke that his boss Calvert M. "Cal" Frederickson had created over the eight years he had occupied his office at Frederickson and Associates. Cal was seated behind his old wooden desk while looking down at a check in his large hands. A man was sitting across from Cal and turned when he heard Tom enter.

"Ah, is this Mr. Donovan?" the man asked.

"Yes it is," Cal said before Tom had a chance to reply. The man stood up and offered his hand to Tom. He was about 6' 2" and 240 pounds.

"Ted Winters," he said. "I own Winters' Janitorial Service."

Tom shook his hand but said nothing.

"I have to thank you for the very thorough job you

did on the matter I brought to Mr. Frederickson," Winters said and looked at Cal and then at Tom. "The information you provided has been very helpful."

A month ago Tom had been assigned by Cal to shadow several of Mr. Winters' employees. Winters had claimed that the employees were stealing from him or otherwise planning to sabotage his business, for whatever reason. He had tracked their movements and photographed them meeting with people outside the company at various locations. All the results had been turned over to Winters.

"Yeah, I guess the Pinkerton's don't do this kind of stuff anymore," Tom said looking back at Winters. He could feel Cal glaring at him.

Winters looked perplexed. "What kind of 'stuff' are you talking about?" he asked. The smile slowly leaving his acne scarred face.

"You know, break up strikes. Stamp out union activity," Tom responded without hesitation

"Donovan," Cal said quietly but firmly.

As Winters realized what Tom was saying he angered quickly. "Hey, fuck you junior," he sputtered. "I just wrote a pretty good size check to your boss here," he said pointing at Cal. "And do you know what it costs to run a business in this state?"

Donovan could tell Winters was the kind of guy who was used to intimidating people but he didn't back down. If anything he leaned closer to him with his left shoulder as he balanced his weight on the balls of his feet. "Well, it can't be too bad," Donovan said with all the righteous indignation he could muster. "Considering you are screwing all the help out of overtime, and the benefits you are taking deductions out for."

"Who do you think you're talking to?" Winters asked, as he turned red with either anger or embarrassment. "Who the hell told you that bullshit?"

"Donovan, that's enough," Cal said rising to his feet.

"Let's just say some things came up during the investigation." Tom's voice was rising steadily. "Pretty much some of the worst kept secrets in your shop."

Winters had turned back to Cal and asked, "Do you treat all your customers this way?"

"As a matter of fact," Tom started again "If it wasn't for you being such an ass-"

"Tom, I said that's enough," Cal yelled, he had come around the desk and placed one of his large hands on Tom's shoulder. Cal looked pretty pissed off. He might have been just as red-faced as Winters if he had been Caucasian. "Out," Cal ordered. "Now."

He turned Tom around and pushed him out of his office. With a glance to Grace, who had surely been listening to everything, he went back in closed the door behind him. Immediately they could hear Winters voice on the other side yelling something about stopping payment on the check and Cal's inaudible reply, either trying to soothe Winters or more likely telling him he better not even dream of doing that.

"Hey?" Grace said looking up at Tom with her blue eyes smiling.

"Yes, Grace?" Tom said, his heartbeat slowing to normal.

"We ran out of coffee. I would go myself but I have to finish these invoices before two o'clock. Would you be a dear and run down to Timmy's and get a can?"

Tom ran his hand over his closely cropped hair. He was coming down and starting to realize what he had just done. "Don't worry Grace, I won't make any more trouble today."

"You will if the old man comes out with that dirt bag and they see you here," she said. "Just disappear for a half hour and come back. We have something else we need you for now that you're clear.

Tom headed to the exterior door.

"Tom?" Grace said.

"I know, don't forget the coffee."

Twenty minutes later Donovan pushed his way back into the office. Grace looked up and was about to say something when Cal's voice boomed out from his office.

"Donovan!"

Donovan took a deep breath and entered Cal's office. Cal was seated behind his weathered wooden desk leaning back in his chair. "Have a seat," Cal said, pointing to one of the wooden chairs in front of his desk.

Donovan sat down and said, "Look boss, I'm sorry but that guy-"

Cal held up a large index finger and said, "Wait on that, I got a couple of questions for you."

Donovan took another deep breath "Okay, what?"

"How long have you worked for me now?"

Tom thought for a second. "About nine months."

"Good. And how long have you been off the police force?"

Tom could feel his face turn red. "It'll be two years in June."

Cal leaned forward in his chair and stared directly at Tom. "Then why are you still acting like a cop?"

Tom shrugged. "What do you want me to say?"

Cal lowered his voice, going into his mentor mode. "I don't want you to say anything. I want you to remember that you are a private investigator, that's it. Somebody hires us to do a job, we do it. We don't ask questions, ever."

"Fuck, Cal," Donovan interrupted.

"Listen." The finger was back up. "I know Winters is a piece of shit, but that piece of shit and others keep the lights on in this office and let us all enjoy the lifestyles we have grown accustomed to."

"He is breaking the law. Crap, he is breaking all kinds of laws: labor, immigration, taxes."

Cal leaned back in his chair. "That is not your concern anymore. You did a good job but you have to learn to let that other stuff go. You can't do anything about it now if you wanted to."

"Bullshit," Donovan said. "I could drop a dime on him to every agency I find in the phone book."

Cal picked up a cigar out of an ashtray he had hidden behind his desk and considered lighting it but then put it back. "Son," he said, "it may be too late for that."

"What do you mean?"

"Word may have already leaked out about Mr. Winters sloppy business practices."

Suddenly Tom understood. "Oh, so you're telling me that in the future I should just keep my mouth shut."

"Bingo," Cal said. "That would be the short version of my deeply nuanced advice to you. Also, my friend, you are being paid to conduct investigations, do surveillance. Anything above and beyond that and you are losing focus and to me that is not money well spent."

Grace knocked at the door and announced, "Mr. Shields is here."

Cal put the ashtray away. "Show him into the conference room," he said. Tom got up to leave. "Hang around Tom. I am going to need some of that newly focused investigative prowess of yours."

CHAPTER 2

Frederickson and Associates occupied the lower front part of a 1930's era brick building on Delaware Avenue. The building had originally been an apartment building with twelve units, but as downtown Buffalo spread out and more storefront space was needed, more and more structures were turned into commercial space. The lower front had been a dentist's office and then a law office. The building had been built to last but was starting to show its age outside and in. Cal Frederickson had made some modest renovations with the help of his cousin; new glass entry door, fresh paint and re-tiled floors, but the old wood doors were still in place and the large wood framed windows too. The office still looked like something from a film noir detective movie.

The 'Conference Room' as Cal called it was actually an extra office at the end of the hall. It contained a small table, four chairs and a laptop hooked up to a flat screen monitor mounted on the wall. As Tom followed Cal in a man in his mid-forties with a medium build and sandy-brown hair stood to meet them. He was dressed casually in a well-made sport coat and button down shirt. He looked vaguely familiar.

"Mr. Shields?" Cal said offering his hand. "I am Cal Frederickson and this is one of my associates, Tom Donovan."

Shields shook both their hands and looked concerned. Finally he spoke. "As I said on the phone, Mr. Frederickson, I had hoped to keep this as quiet as possible. This is a very personal matter."

It hit Donovan where he had seen Shields before. He had been on the news recently. One of the local hospitals had turned down a large donation from Shields due to the nature of his business. Shields was the owner of *Showgirls Gentlemen's Club*, a high end strip club, but a strip club nonetheless. The press seemed to be split over whether Shields's intentions had been truly altruistic or just a PR stunt. He had opened his club just outside the city and some of the residents at first were up in arms. But in the end money talks and after all the angry speeches at town board meetings about the decay of society, and assurances from the club's representatives the club would be an honorable business (and tax payer) *Showgirls* was allowed to open.

Cal directed them all to chairs and made introductions. "This is Mr. Donovan. He is my lead investigator."

This was news to Tom. Just an hour ago he thought he might be on his way to being an ex-investigator.

"He will be doing a lot of the legwork for this," Cal continued. "And I can assure you he will handle this with complete confidentiality and discretion." He threw glance at Tom. "Now as I understand it, this is in regards to your wife?"

Shields thought for a moment and then looked up from his hands at Cal then Tom. He regained his composure and confidence.

"Yes," he started. "I am afraid we have been fighting lately and then last night she left home and didn't come back."

"So then you haven't called the police?" Cal asked while starting to take notes on a legal pad.

"No," Shields said. "She told me she was leaving."

"Do you have any idea where she might have gone? Does she have any family?"

"She has a sister here in town but she didn't go there," Shields responded.

"You've spoken to the sister?" Cal asked, one eye brow raised.

"I called her today," Shields said, almost a whisper. "We have a good relationship and I don't think she would lie to me."

Tom noticed that Shields seemed confident on the surface, but there was something off about him that he couldn't put his finger on.

"Do you have the address?" Cal continued.

Shields pushed a 9 x 11 manila envelope across the table towards Cal. "It's in here," he said. "With all of the other things you requested, pictures, personal papers."

"Any other family or friends you can think of?" Cal asked.

"Not locally, her mother died while she was in school and her step father moved out of the area shortly after. They never heard from him after he left town."

Tom decided to jump in. "What makes you think she's still in town?"

Shields turned to face Tom with his chin up, his eyes cold, it seemed to Tom. "She called me last night at home," he stated. "She had left her cell phone at the house and I didn't recognize the number but it was from a 716 area code."

Cal interjected, "Do you have the phone number she called from?"

"I called it back three times and got no answer," Shields answered. "Then I called back a fourth time and got an 'out of service' message. She might have had one of those throw away phones."

"What did she say when she called you?" Cal asked.

Shields looked down at his hands and responded quietly, "She said she was sorry, but that I wasn't who she thought I was when we got married." He hesitated slightly. "I told her we should talk about it but she said she was tying up a few loose ends and then leaving town."

They were all quiet for a minute. There was something about Shields' body language that didn't sit well with Tom.

Cal broke the silence. "Mr. Shields, I know this is a deeply personal matter, but we need as much background as you can give us." He leaned back in his chair and placed his pen on the pad. "What were you two arguing about?"

Shields looked up again and answered, "The club mostly. She hated it, the idea of it." He gazed towards the window even though the shade was closed. "She's no radical feminist, but she says it demeans women and feeds into the worst nature of men."

"Did this come up before you opened the club?" Tom asked. From the corner of his eye he saw Cal glance at him.

"If it did, I'm afraid I didn't take it seriously. And that's on me," he said looking at Tom sharply.

Cal cleared his throat and said, "Mr. Shields, as a precaution I have to ask you, in the event we do locate your wife, what do you plan on doing?"

"What do you mean?" Shields asked, slightly surprised.

"All I mean," Cal began, "is that when we enter into a contract with you to work as your agent, we will do everything to fulfill our part of the contract as long as we know the result of our investigation will not result in a crime."

"What?" Shields gasped. Tom couldn't tell if it was either true indignation or some concocted reaction.

Cal lowered his voice, but as only he could, maintained his authority. "Standard procedure for a domestic case, Mr. Shields. Nothing personal about you but we don't want to be involved in a situation that will result in the commission of a crime. I don't know a better way to put it. I have seen more than a few of these family things get out of hand."

Shields furrowed his brow and looked back down at his hands on the table. He seemed to be thinking.

"In other words," Tom began, "does your wife have anything to be afraid of?" He regretted saying it as soon as it came out of his mouth. He couldn't bring himself to look at Cal.

Shields looked up at Tom and shook his head in disbelief. "No," he said and then turned to Cal. "My God, you think just because I own a gentlemen's club I'm some kind of violent pimp?"

"Mr. Shields," Cal said calmly, trying to defuse the situation. "I'm sure Mr. Donavan did not intend to imply any such thing."

"No, I will answer the question," Shields went on, raising his right hand. "Donna and I have been married for twelve years. We've been though a lot together. She stuck with me through a lot of ups and downs. I love her and wouldn't do anything to hurt her."

Cal sat back in his seat and glanced at Tom as if to prompt him.

Tom inhaled and said, "Mr. Shields, I apologize if that question seemed out of line."

Shields seemed to think about this. Cal picked it up from there.

"What happens between you and your wife is your business Mr. Shields," he said calmly. "But please try to understand that I have to protect the reputation of my business as well as my license." Cal sat back in his chair again and folded his hands in front of his stomach. He looked directly at Shields. "Eight years ago, when I first got into this business I had a gentleman hire me to find out if his wife was cheating on him." Cal paused and looked away from Shields, turning his chair slightly to the window. "Turns out she was. The day after I turned over the photographs to my client he beat his wife to death with a golf club."

The room was silent. Shields squirmed in his seat a little. Tom sat motionless, relieved that Cal had, more or less, smoothed things out.

"I understand," Shields finally said. "But believe me, I just want to find my wife and talk to her, apologize. Hell, if she wants me to I'll sell the club. But I can't tell her anything until I find her." He was almost pleading.

"Of course," Cal said. "Tell you what, we can certainly look into this. If you still want to engage us we have a short, standard contract."

"How much do you need to get started?" Shields

asked quickly.

"Typically we bill by the hour."

"I'll sign on one condition," Shields said, regaining his earlier polish.

"Sir?"

"I have a five thousand dollar check in my pocket if you can look me in the eye and promise to make finding my wife your top priority. That is on top of your standard rate."

"Mr. Shields, I don't think…" Cal began.

Shields wasn't done. "And another five thousand dollars if you can find her before she leaves town."

"I can't make any promises," Cal replied firmly.

"I'm not asking you to," Shields said. "I just want to talk to her. And I want you to give it everything you have."

Cal rocked back in his chair. Tom could read him after nine months of employment and knew he was pretending to think.

"It is unusual," Cal said, stretching it out. "Given the circumstances though I can assure you we will do everything we can to find your wife." He stood up and extended his hand to Shields. "I will have Grace put an addendum on the contract and we can get that signed."

Tom rose also and shook hands with Shields. "Right this way," Cal said to Shields, moving him towards the door. As soon as they crossed the threshold he heard Cal say to him. "You go ahead, I forgot my notes." Then Cal's large frame filled up the doorway again. Tom didn't know if he should duck or run.

"Damn, you learn slow," Cal said frowning.

"Sorry boss, it's just that guy, I don't know," Tom said

"I know, something's up with that boy," Cal replied picking up his legal pad. "In the meantime, I want you to start going through that envelope and see if anything jumps out at you." He turned to leave.

"I didn't know about that guy killing his wife with a golf club either," Tom said in an almost dismissive manner.

Cal turned around to face Tom and lowered his voice to a near whisper. "That's because I just made it up." He winked then turned and walked out.

Tom took the envelope to the cramped office he shared with Sherry Palkowski, who was out running down witnesses for a lawyer friend of Cal's. He opened the envelope and let the contents slide out onto his desk.

The first things he saw were the photographs. Donna Shields was a very pretty woman, shoulder length brown hair, blue eyes and a brilliant smile. There were copies of some vacation photos taken someplace tropical and a picture of Donna at a charity event standing next to her husband and the mayor. The best picture was a close up of her at what appeared to be the Shield's home by a large fireplace. She was smiling but there was something in her eyes.

There was a knock on the door. It was Grace. "Tom, there's a guy here by the name of Smitty here to see you," she said.

"Who?" Tom asked.

Grace looked back at him. "He said his name was Smitty, he said it like he was somebody you knew."

Tom followed Grace out to the reception area, racking his brain. Who the hell was Smitty? High school classmate? Gold Gloves? A cop?

As he got to Grace's Desk a burly man in an overcoat stood up and smiled. Tom had never seen him before in his life.

Tom Donovan?" the man said thrusting out his hand. "Jim Smith."

"I'm drawing a blank. Have we met?" Tom asked.

"Not 'til today, but you gotta check this out." With his left hand he handed Tom a sheaf of papers. The smile disappeared from Smitty's face. "You've been served," he said gravely.

Tom felt his anger start to rise but before he could say anything Smitty was out the door.

"What was that all about?" Grace asked.

Tom opened the papers up and glanced through them. He had been expecting something like this for a long time.

"I've been named in a civil suit for the wrongful death of Derrick Trent."

CHAPTER 3

Two years earlier.

It was a cold night for late March, even by Buffalo standards. A few stray flakes fell out of the dark sky as Tom and his Partner Joe Walczak climbed into the unmarked Crown Victoria.

"Now what?" Joe asked putting the key into the ignition.

Tom's mind was racing and he was trying to get himself to think rationally. He was finding it extremely difficult. "Let's head back to the division," he said.

They had just left the intensive care unit of the medical center. Tom had gotten a tip that a sixteen-year-old girl he knew had been admitted and was in pretty rough shape. He had just endured ten minutes of a hysterical mother blaming him for putting her daughter in there.

"What are you thinking?" Joe asked, accelerating onto Grider Street.

"I'm thinking we need to ditch this car first," Tom responded, staring straight ahead.

"And why would we do that?"

"I want to talk to Trent and we're not getting close to him in this thing. It kind of sticks out down at the projects."

Joe looked over and said, "Bad idea Tom. Really bad." He nearly sideswiped a pedestrian. "Jesus, you don't even know it was him."

For the past two months Tom and Joe had been assigned to assist the Narcotics Squad. The gang known as NBH had been making inroads toward cornering the drug market on the city's East Side. One of the higher ups was Derrick 'Terror' Trent, and the cops were trying to gather as much information on him as possible. Information was hard to come by on the East Side. The NBH and other street gangs ruled through fear and intimidation: "snitches get stitches" was a general rule of thumb in the neighborhoods. That, and a large portion of the locals didn't trust the cops either.

Alicia Simmons's only crime was that she called 911 one night when her brother got roughed up outside of her family's Krupp Ave home. Tom had shown up with the uniforms and tried to take a statement. Alicia had said that her brother was being harassed by members of the NBH for reasons her brother wouldn't tell her or the police. Retribution was swift and thorough. Alicia had a broken eye socket, broken ribs and a collapsed lung.

Tom looked back at Joe and said, "Yeah, well if it wasn't him it was one of his crew."

"I don't think Captain Hillis is going to like us

going half cocked into the McKinley Projects with blood in our eyes," Joe responded as he looked around, not afraid, but concerned.

Tom was trying to measure his breath and stay calm. "So we let this guy just beat up whoever calls the cops?"

Joe thought about this and then said, "No, but you better promise me that this won't get out of hand."

Tom looked out of his window. "Look, you don't even have to come. I just want to talk to Trent."

Joe laughed. "Right. Number one. do you think I am going to let you go into the projects by yourself? And number two, do you think I am going to let you do something stupid and get yourself or somebody else killed?"

"We are just going to talk," Tom said. "Nobody's getting killed."

Tom gave a glance in Joe's direction. Even though it was still cold inside the car he could see traces of perspiration on Joe's brow.

Twenty minutes later they were sitting outside of Derrick Trent's apartment building. The housing authority had rules about renting to convicted felons like Trent. But the squad had learned that the unit was rented out in Trent's aunt's name, yet no one had ever seen his aunt enter or leave the building. The wind off the lake whipped and rocked Tom's SUV. It was freezing inside the vehicle. He turned the engine off so there would be no visible exhaust and had also cracked the windows so they wouldn't fog up.

Almost an hour had gone by and only a handful of people had come into view, none of them approaching the building. Tom could sense Joe getting restless.

Joe said, "You think he may be laying low somewhere else?"

"Could be," Tom told him, checking his side view mirror. "But Trent, if nothing else, is a ballsy son of a bitch. Not like him to run and hide."

"Are you sure you don't want to call A division, let them know we are on their beat?"

Tom sighed. "I know we should but I think the fewer people here the better for the time being. Holy shit! There he is," he exclaimed as he reached for the door handle.

Joe peered down the dark walkway at two men moving from the opposite direction towards the front door of the unit. "Are you sure?"

"Yep, I recognize the walk," Tom said and he was out of the car.

Joe was already on the sidewalk as Tom came around the car. "Who's that with him?"

"I don't know. Hard to tell in this shitty light," Tom said as he unzipped his jacket.

Joe saw him and asked, "We just came to talk, right?" His tone was grave.

"I did, but I can't speak for Trent or his friend."

Joe seemed to see the wisdom in that and unbuttoned

his coat.

The wind picked up and the sound of the trucks rolling by on the nearby I-190 shook through the night. "Trent," Tom yelled. The two men apparently didn't hear his as they entered the building.

"Come on," Tom said. "I want to catch up before he gets into auntie's apartment." He broke into a jog.

"What floor is he on?" Joe asked.

"Basement."

They reached the door and threw it open. The stairs leading down to the basement apartments were to the right. As soon as they got halfway down the stairs they saw him, Derrick 'Terror' Trent, with a set of keys in his hand looking up the stairs at them. He was with another man, black, early thirties in a thick black down jacket.

"Who the fuck are you?" asked the man in the down jacket.

"It's the Buffalo Po-lice," Trent said maintaining his stare at Tom and Joe.

Black Jacket shifted his weight and dropped his right hand to his thigh. "What do you want?" he said.

Something was off. Tom had never seen this guy before and he didn't look like your average gang-banger. It had been speculated that the NBH was trying to expand into other cities. Could this guy be out of town muscle maybe?

"Just want to speak to Derrick here for a few," Tom said. Over his shoulder he could sense Joe tensing up. He knew Joe was fearless, he had seen him get into some pretty good scrapes since they had become partners.

"You got a warrant?" Black Jacket asked, no fear, no concern.

"Are you his fucking lawyer?" Tom asked.

"So you're just here to bust his balls?" Black Jacket responded with a smile. "Or are you here to shake him down?"

"Fuck you," Joe said over Tom's shoulder. Tom was a little surprised. Joe was usually the calm one.

The hallway seemed very warm all of a sudden and the air stagnant. Derrick turned to his friend and said, "C'mon, they ain't got shit." He put his key in the lock and turned it.

Tom took a step down. Black Jacket tensed. "Alicia Simmons," Tom said raising his voice.

Trent stopped, turned and looked Tom in the eye. "Never heard of the bitch," he said slowly.

Tom could hear Joe step down behind him. He knew his partner was trying to get off to his left to divide their attention. Black Jacket seemed to sense this and stared daggers at Joe. Joe could only move so far, the hallway was narrow and there was and old bike and shopping cart outside the unit across the hall.

"Well, when she wakes up," Tom began, "you better pray that she doesn't give the detective waiting outside her room your description. Who knows? Maybe her family and neighbors have had enough of your bullshit and are ready to get rid of you."

Trent let a slight smile cross his face. "Anything else, officer?" He cracked the door slightly.

"You fellahs should probably get going now," Black Jacket said he put his hand on Trent's shoulder. "He's got nothing to say."

"Tom, you smell that?" Joe asked.

Tom picked up on where Joe was going. "Yep. The distinct smell of marijuana emanating from this public housing unit." Tom stepped right up to Trent's side.

"Bullshit," Trent said.

"Fuck this," Black Jacket said. His right hand moved up his side.

"Gun," Joe yelled.

Tom pushed Trent hard into Black jacket as he reached to his belt for his 9mm. Black Jacket had drawn a gun and was raising it when Trent crashed into him. The gun roared and the noise blocked out every other sound in the hallway. Out of the corner of his eye Tom saw Joe double over and fall to the floor. Black jacket pushed Trent off of him and through the apartment door. Before he could say anything Tom shot Black Jacket in the dead center of his forehead.

Tom looked over his shoulder at Joe, who was lying on his side with his hand over a hole in his abdomen. His eyes were open but seemed to be out of focus.

"Joe," Tom yelled, his ears still ringing from the two shots in such a confined space.

Nothing. Joe just looked at nothing and breathed irregularly. Tom turned towards the door Trent had disappeared though. He crouched low and pushed the door the rest of the way open.

"Trent," Tom yelled. Nothing, only ringing. He moved slowly into the cramped living room. There was a light on in the kitchen. Tom glanced in and saw no one there. He turned towards the hallway to the bedrooms. His heart was pounding and he felt like throwing up thinking about Joe, possibly dying out in the filthy hallway.

No more yelling, he thought. The next time this guy hears me he'll put a bullet in me. He passed the bathroom and was just about to look into the door on his left when he heard a sound off to his right. It sounded like a round being chambered.

Tom quietly stepped across the hall and put his hand on the partially opened door. Suddenly from inside the room he heard glass shatter. Shit, he thought. Trent was going for the window. Tom kicked the door open and ducked into the darkened room with his weapon in a two handed grip.

"Trent!" he yelled.

Trent was silhouetted standing on the bed where he had been trying to break the window. He turned quickly when Tom called out. Tom caught the glimmer of something metal in Trent's right hand. With his adrenaline on overdrive and his heart pumping in his chest Tom squeezed off three shots in Trent's direction.

The combination of the dark room and the muzzle flash temporarily blinded Tom and he waited for the bullet or bullets from Trent's gun to rip into his own body. As his eyes adjusted and the smoke started to rise he saw Trent leaning back into the wall and then fall face first on the bed. The dank room was now filled with ringing and the smell of cordite. Tom couldn't catch his breath. He kept his gun pointed towards the bed as he sidestepped back to the doorway to find the light switch. He flipped the switch and the dim light from a ceiling fixture barely cut through the remaining smoke.

"Trent!" Tom yelled again as he moved towards the bed, never taking his aim off the fallen man.

Trent was lying on his stomach with his head tuned to the side. He was making a rasping, gurgling sound as blood poured from his mouth. One of Tom's shots had hit him in the throat, he was fading fast. Tom looked at Trent's right hand and there was no gun.

"What the fuck?" Tom said out loud. He looked over the side of the bed and lying on the floor was a stainless steel faucet tap for a bathroom sink. Trent must have been using it to try and break the window. "No fucking way," he said to himself.

Footsteps in the hall. It would be a patrol from A

Division. Tom backed out of the bedroom.

"Freeze, Federal Officers!"

It wasn't A Division. Two large men in black vests with DEA emblazoned over their chests were in the apartment with automatic weapons pointed at Tom. "Drop the gun now," one of them was yelling.

Tom was dazed. He held his gun at his side and tried to make sense of it all.

The agent on the left moved forward, he was a big guy with his shaved head glistening with sweat. "Did you shoot him?" he yelled.

"He's in the bedroom," Tom said.

No, not him asshole, did you shoot Carl?" the agent yelled and practically had his gun barrel in Tom's face.

"Drop the gun," the other agent added. He was a half step behind.

"Who the fuck is Carl?" Tom asked. Suddenly he remembered that Joe was lying out in the hall with a bullet in his gut. "And who the fuck are you?" Tom yelled to no one in particular, the gravity of the situation starting become real.

"You just shot a Federal agent you prick," the bald agent said through clenched teeth.

Tom dropped his gun, but the bald agent kept his pointed at Tom's head.

"A dirty fucking cop," the bald agent growled.

"Hey, my partner is lying in that hall," Tom sneered.

"And your buddy Carl is the one who put a slug in him." Tom was glad he had dropped his gun, he felt his blood rising. He knew he had to calm down and take care of his partner.

The bald agent wasn't swayed and it really looked like he was ready to shoot. Tom thought this was a pretty crappy way to go, on account of some piece of shit drug dealer. And he was going to take poor Joe with him.

"Casey, lower your weapon," another, older agent had entered the apartment. He pointed to Tom and said, "Anderson, cuff that man and get him out of here."

The bald agent lowered his weapon slightly as the one named Anderson put his handcuffs on Tom. When the older agent started barking orders into his radio Casey leaned into Tom's face and said, "This is your lucky night asshole."

As Anderson pushed him past Casey, Tom said, "Yeah, fucking night of my life, dickhead."

When they made the hallway the paramedics were working on Joe. They had an oxygen mask on him and Tom could see he was breathing. All of the relief he felt was at once taken away when he looked over and saw the DEA agent he had shot lying still with no-one working on him, waiting for the medical examiner.

The next six months were the worst of Tom's life. Joe lived but the bullet had severed his spinal chord and he would never walk again. It turned out Trent was being squeezed by the DEA to turn over on some very powerful people in Chicago. His contact, the dead agent, was just about to seal the deal. The DEA had not informed Buffalo PD since they hadn't expected two cops to crash the party. They wanted Tom's head, but after the case was heard by a grand jury Tom was cleared in the shooting. What he wasn't cleared with was the court of public opinion. Even though Trent was a convicted felon, the DEA did Tom no favors when they claimed that Trent was turning over a new leaf. It also came to light that Trent had been the sole supporter for his late brother's two children, one of whom was special needs. That coupled with the fact that Trent was unarmed when Tom shot him made Tom a pariah in the black community's eyes.

The only thing that may have saved him was that Alicia Simmons had testified that before she lost consciousness she heard one of her attackers say, "This is what you get when you fuck with Terror."

Ironically it was the first time in ten years as a policeman that Tom had discharged his weapon in the line of duty. But between the death of a Federal agent and the shooting of an unarmed man, "You're lucky you're just losing your job." the Assistant Commissioner told him the day they took his badge. His union rep told him just about the same thing.

Tom was done as a cop.

CHAPTER 4

Tom and Cal were back in Cal's office. Cal was scanning the summons that Tom had been handed twenty minutes before. Without looking up Cal asked, "Are you going to use Stanley again?"

Robert M. Stanley was the attorney Tom had hired to represent him for the double shooting that had ended his career as a policeman.

"No offense boss, but I can't afford him in my current financial position." Tom said.

Cal glanced up. "None taken. I heard he is pretty expensive."

It was true. Stanley had helped Tom navigate through the legal quagmire he had created, but it had pretty much eaten up his life savings and the registration on his shiny new SUV in the process.

"Well, pretty obvious you are going to need an attorney and soon," Cal said looking back down at the summons. "I could recommend somebody."

Tom smiled weakly and said, "Who? One of the ambulance chasers we work for?"

Cal glared at him over his reading glasses. "I

should remind you that it's bad form to bite the hand that feeds you." He put the papers down and sat back. "No, I have some people who owe me a favor or two. If you can promise me one thing I will make a couple of calls."

"What's that?" Tom asked.

"You prove to me that you can watch your mouth and your temper," Cal replied. "A lot of this is going to be tried in the press, unfortunately, and you have a history of shooting yourself in the foot."

Tom flushed slightly. The last thing he thought he needed was a lecture. But in the end he decided to bite his tongue. "I would appreciate the help," he said.

"Good," Cal replied rising from his chair. "Glad to hear it. Are you still up for the Shields thing?"

Tom stood up also. "Yeah, no problem there. I need to keep busy."

Cal looked directly at Tom and said with undue gravity, "Think you can stay focused? This could get interesting."

"No problem, boss. If anything I think I need this right now."

"Yeah, I know what you mean," Cal answered.

Tom went back to his office and resumed going through the contents of the envelope that Gary Shields had left. He went through the documents without finding anything particularly useful and put everything back in the envelope with the exception of two of the pictures of

Shields' wife, which he put in his coat pocket. Sherry Palkowski walked in. She put a large shoulder bag and a digital camera on her desk and took her coat off.

"Tough day, huh?" she said looking towards Tom.

"Eh, kind of been waiting for it to happen," Tom replied.

Sherry stood about 5' 7" and had medium length blond hair, which she had pulled back today. Tom and Sherry had an odd relationship; Sherry aspired to be a cop, and Tom had been one, and Tom suspected that Sherry believed he'd thrown it all away. She had never come out and said as much but Tom could sense that she kept her distance due to the fact he had left the police force under a cloud. Sherry had taken the exam and done well but the numbers were against her. The city had cut back on it's hiring and just having a criminal justice degree didn't carry that much weight. Also Tom had the stigma of being a 'legacy hire' due to the fact that his maternal uncle Sam was a Captain in D District.

"How was your expedition?" he said changing the subject.

"Pretty good," she said gesturing to the camera. "The place is an injury lawyer's wet dream."

Tom picked up the envelope and started to leave. "Do you know if Brian is in?" he asked. Brian Dinkle was the agency's resident computer nerd.

"I heard music from his office when I went by but

that doesn't mean anything," Sherry said sitting down. "Hey Tom?"

"Yeah," he said turning back.

"You need any help with the Trent thing let me know."

Tom was surprised but tried not to show it. "Thanks Sherry, I appreciate that."

Brian was in his office. He was the only associate of the agency to have his own space. Primarily because he had it filled with computer equipment, much of which seemed to not be functioning, and secondly because he was a tad eccentric.

There was one other office that the two part time guys, two retired cops named Adams and Willis shared.

Cal had hired Brian a few years back after the company that he worked for had hired Cal to do a security sweep. The company's management suspected that someone outside the company had been looking into their financial records and wanted to know who. It had turned out that Brian had been passed over for a promotion and a raise so out of spite he had hacked into the CFO's computer and harvested some of the companies more questionable record keeping and was posting it on line. The only reason he had been caught was when Cal had tripped him up during an interview and Brian, rather proudly, then confessed. Rather than press charges and have their dirty laundry aired, the company paid Brian a year's salary and installed a new firewall. Cal Frederickson, never at a loss to spot talent when he saw it, hired Brian six months later.

"Major Tom," Brian said turning the music down when he noticed Tom standing over his desk. "What's up?"

"You busy Brian?"

"Why, you need me to dig up something on Trent's friends and family?" he asked raising an eyebrow. "Or how about something on the Good Reverend Mason?"

Christ, Tom thought. Does everybody know about this? "No, none of that," he replied trying to control his frustration and handed Brian the manila envelope. "Runaway bride. Not much in there but the basics: drivers license number, social security, marriage license. I wondered if you could poke around in cyberspace and see it you come across something of interest. The husband claims she's still in town but I have my doubts."

"Okay, will do. Are you going to be here for a while?" It was five-o-clock. Tom had forgotten Brian seldom kept what people thought of as regular hours.

"Ah, no, I've got a little personal business to take care of." Tom wanted to break the news of the lawsuit to his mother before she saw it on the early news. "If you find something call me on my cell."

"Roger that," Brian said. He pulled his chair in front of the large monitor on his cluttered desk. Tom turned to leave.

Tom thought of something that was bothering him.

"I hate to ask this Brian," he trailed off.

Brian looked up. "What is it?"

"If you would, take a look at the husband. I got a weird vibe from the guy."

"Ah, the plot thickens," Brian said. "Are we also reporting this to the boss?"

The kid was almost too smart.

"Ah, run whatever you find by me first."

"Absolutely," Brian said with a wry smile and gave Tom the OK sign and went back to his computer.

Tom felt drained as he pushed his way through the door of the office building out on to Delaware Ave. He turned towards the direction where his car was parked when he noticed the ten-year-old Cadillac parked in front of the fire hydrant. The passenger side window of the Caddy rolled down. "Tommy!" A familiar voice yelled out. It was Whitey Brennan, an old family acquaintance.

Tom leaned on the passenger side and looked in at Whitey. "Hey Whitey, what brings you all the way out of the First Ward?"

Whitey killed the engine and smiled his tobacco stained smile. He was a large man with a shock of white hair and a crooked nose. "I came to see you, ya little shit," he said and laughed a little and then the smile seemed to leave his face. "Tommy, Hugh tells me that you changed your phone number and he can't get a hold of you."

Hugh Donovan was Tom's paternal Grandfather.

Their relationship became somewhat strained after Tom Sr. died, somewhat hostile when Tom became a cop and non-existent after Tom was kicked off the police force.

Tom thought for a second. "Whitey, you were my dad's best friend, you've known me all my life. You've known Hugh even longer. You gotta believe me when I tell you, I have nothing to say to him."

Whitey shook his head sadly, never taking his eyes from Tom's. "You know the old man isn't going to be around forever," he said. "He just wants to talk to you. He worries about you, believe it or not. It broke his heart what happened to your dad. And the fact that you two are estranged is really bothering him, I can tell."

Tom responded, "Why would he be worried about me?"

"The old man still has some connections. He hears things," Whitey said looking out through his windshield. "He knows about the lawsuit."

Of course he does, Tom Thought. He wasn't in the mood to argue.

"Alright, are you going back to the bar?" Tom asked.

"Yep, closing up tonight. Is there a message?"

Tom straightened slightly up and took a step back. "Tell him I'll be in to see him in the morning."

"Ah, bless ya Tommy," Whitey said, smiling as he turned the engine over.

"God knows I need it," Tom said tapping the top of the car.

CHAPTER 5

By the time he arrived at his mother's house on Taunton Place she had already seen the news. Through misty eyes she told him about the press conference televised from the steps of the courthouse. Reverend Ezra Mason, the community activist, and prominent attorney George Frangos had outlined their lawsuit against Tom, his former partner Joe Walczak, the Buffalo Police Department and the DEA. Frangos had made the legal part of the statement and then it was Rev. Mason's turn to shine. He had elaborated on how even though Derrick Trent was a young man with a violent and checkered past he had been attempting to turn his life around. And who were a few rogue cops to act as judge, jury and executioner? He even alleged poor young Derrick may have been targeted because he was going to turn over evidence he had on some crooked cops. Frangos finally pulled the plug on the proceedings before they got out of hand and that was all Tom's mother could take. She had turned the TV off and just sat looking out the front window.

Tom's Mother, Rosalie Dipietro Donovan, had seen her share of misery. Tom's sister had been killed by a drunk driver when she was ten years old while riding her bike. Then her husband, Big Tom, had died when he drove his car into the Buffalo River the day before his thirty seventh birthday, leaving her unemployed and uninsured with fifteen year old Tom to deal with.

Rose's parents had never really approved of Big Tom and they made no secret of it. The Donovan family was widely known to be involved in bookmaking and other dubious enterprises in South Buffalo. Big Tom and Rose met at a night club on Hertel Avenue and that meeting sparked a Rust Belt version of Romeo and Juliet.

The first one to reach out to Rose after Big Tom's death was her brother Samuel. Sam Dipietro, then a lieutenant in the Buffalo PD moved his sister and her son into the house he owned on Taunton, He helped Rose find a job as a secretary at a local Catholic school and became a mentor to Tom.

Rose seemed to have put some of the past pain behind her and was doing well until the McKinley Project shooting. The legal ordeal and Tom's losing his job seemed to age her rapidly. She tried to hide it from Tom, but there were times he could see the pain in her eyes.

Tom spent the better part of an hour telling his mother it was all just a cash grab by the plaintiffs and a photo op for Mason and Frangos. She had recovered somewhat and Tom knew she was trying to put on a brave face for him. Tom felt awful though, like he had let her down again.

The air was tight in her living room and he felt like he was suffocating. Feeling guilty, he excused himself and said he would call her tomorrow.

As Tom walked out to his car his cell phone buzzed he checked the caller ID, it was the office.

"Major Tom, it's Brian."

"Hey, yeah Brian. Didn't expect to hear from you so soon."

"Oh, this is just a preliminary there'll be some more to come after hours," Brian said.

Tom didn't ask what that meant. He didn't want to know

His phone buzzed again with another call. "Hang on Brian," he said. Tom checked the number it was his Uncle Sam. He had to take it.

"Shit, Brian can I call you back?"

"Sure, I'll be here for a while."

Tom punched the button and said, "Uncle Sam?"

"Hey kid, how ya doing?"

"I'm alright, all things considered."

"Did you talk to your mom?"

"Yeah, I just left the house."

"Is she OK?"

Tom hesitated, then said, "She's pretty upset. I ran out of things to tell her."

Sam replied, "It's understandable; you have a lot on your mind. I'm going to head over there in a little while."

"Thanks Sam," Tom said, relieved.

"Keep your chin up kid. This will blow over eventually."

Tom climbed into his car. "Yeah, I hope so."

"You got a lawyer in mind?" Sam asked.

Tom hesitated for a moment again. "Cal is making a few calls."

The line was silent. Even though Cal was an ex-cop himself Sam had never seemed to like the idea of Tom working for him. There was some kind of animosity between the two that had never been explained to Tom.

"Well Ok," Sam finally said. "You could always go with Bob Stanley again. And don't worry about the money. I have some stashed away your Aunt Diane doesn't know about. It's sort of a rainy day fund."

Tom closed his eyes. His Uncle had been sticking his neck out for him since he was a teenager. He already felt deeply indebted to the man and didn't want to think about having Sam bail him out once again. He measured his breath and said, "Thanks, Uncle Sam. I'll have to think about that."

"What's to think about? We're family," Sam said, rather impatiently.

Tom tried to back pedal. "Sam listen, I love you. You've been like a father to me since dad died. I just need a night to process this, OK?"

Tom could hear his uncle take a deep breath over

the phone. "Alright kid. No worries. Just make sure I don't have to come looking for you."

"Absolutely. Listen, I'm working tonight and I've gotta call I have to make."

"Alright Tommy. You be careful."

"Will do. Goodnight." Tom clicked off.

He punched the call back number for the office, it went to voice mail. He looked up Brian's cell phone number in his contact list and called it. Brian answered on the first ring.

"Brian, sorry about that. Are you on your way home?"

"No boyo," Brian answered. "I'm still at the office. I kinda lose track of time when I am doing research, especially when it's as interesting as your Mr. And Mrs. Shields."

Tom took his notebook out of his coat pocket. "Really? You came up with something already."

Tommy Boy, I have the feeling we are just scratching the surface," Brian said and then chomped into what sounded like an apple.

Tom pulled the phone away from his ear while Brian chewed for a moment. "Alright, what do you have on Donna Shields so far?" Tom asked.

"She's the boring one," Brian said swallowing. Then he began to read, "Born Donna Lynn Hauser 1978, Graduated Immaculata Academy 1995. Then off to College at University of Rochester, graduated from there 1999, Dean's list all four years. BA in business. Got a job back here at one of the big banks downtown. Married to Gary F. Shields in 2000. Quit her job in 2003. No kids, never arrested, pretty boring existence."

Tom frowned. "What about her family, anything there?" he asked.

"Not much." Brian paused. "Father died when she was five. Her mother remarried when she was eight. Some guy named David Stanton. Mother passed away when she was away at the U of R, leukemia." Tom could hear Brian scrolling down on his keyboard. "Not much on the step-dad. Almost looks like he just kind of disappeared. She has a half-sister who lives out in Clarence. Let's see, Angela Cryer, age twenty four, married, one kid, she's a dental hygienist."

"Hmm," Tom said, slightly frustrated. "Not a lot there. How about the husband?"

"Ah," Brian said. "This is where it gets interesting." Tom could hear the sound of a few keys being struck. "Gary Francis Shields, born June 1968 in Cleveland Ohio. Public schools. Got a Scholarship to Canisius College. Graduated in '89. Went to work as a financial planner at a local firm. And here's where it gets interesting." Brian paused to build the suspense.

"Go on," Tom said.

"He lost his broker's license in '93 and got shitcanned from the firm."

"Why?" Tom asked.

"From what I could dredge up from the old news files he was accused of running a somewhat complicated Ponzi scheme," Brian said. "It kind of fell off the press's radar after a few months when the Feds said that he had made it appear just legitimate enough that they might not be able to indict him." Brian paused. "Hey Tommy, I have to ask you something."

"Ask me what?"

"There is more about this guy but it just dawned on me, you are looking for the wife, right?"

"And you want to know why I wanted you to look at the husband too?" Tom asked.

"Bingo," Brian said. "You know how Calvert gets about discretion and all that stuff. He is already riding my ass for some freelance stuff I was doing on the company computer."

"Yeah, I got a lecture on focus and friendly customer service today," Tom said and thought for a second. "Say as little to the boss about this as possible. If he has a problem with it I will just explain that I was following my keen investigative instincts and wanted kind of a big picture look at it."

Brian chuckled and took another bite of his apple. With a mouthful he said, "Sounds like bullshit, but OK. It's your ass."

"Is there more about Shields?" Tom asked.

"Yup." Brian swallowed. "Somehow he had enough capital to start flipping houses in some of the more disadvantaged neighborhoods. Actually made a killing in it. He then expanded into commercial real estate in 2006. His firm is called Advantage Realty."

"Shit, they have signs up all over the city," Tom said writing in the notebook.

"All over the area," Brian added. "From Niagara Falls to the PA line."

"What about the strip club?"

Brian typed something in. "Yeah, interesting thing about that. It's the only business interest he has that isn't in his name."

"What do you mean?"

"Everything associated with the Showgirls Gentlemen's Club is in the name of Donna Lynn Hauser: liquor license, lease, ASCAP registration."

Tom looked up and pulled away from the curb. "That is odd."

"Not really," Brian responded. "Given the husband's shady past."

"No, I get that part. The thing is Shields told me his wife hated the whole concept of the strip club."

"Gentlemen's Club," Brian corrected him in a sarcastic tone.

"Yeah, whatever. It just strikes me as odd that she

would sign all that paperwork if she was so dead set against it."

Brian thought for a moment. "Yeah, I guess that is weird."

"Is there any dirt on the club?"

"Nope," Brian said. "They pay all their taxes, have a good credit rating. Only a couple of police calls since they opened including one last night."

Tom looked up. "Really? What time last night?"

Brian clicked to another screen. "Police blotter says they got a call at 10:30, possible fight in the parking lot. Nothing going on when they rolled in. None of the employees saw anything."

"Hmm," Tom muttered. "I would love to ask Shields why everything would be in his wife's maiden name." Then he realized, "Shit, I have no contact information for Shields."

"Do you want his unlisted number?" Brian said. "I've got it right here."

Tom was pretty sure that Gary Shields's unlisted phone number wasn't in the envelope that he gave to Brian and he knew better than to ask how he got it. He pulled over on Hertel Avenue and picked up his notebook. "Sure, let me have it."

Chapter 6

It was 8:20 PM when Tom walked into his upper flat apartment on St. James. The first thing he saw when he walked in was the rack of CDs next to the spot where the stereo used to be. His ex-girlfriend, Erica, had taken the compact stereo with her when she moved out two months before.

Erica and Tom had been dating for four years, living together for three. She had stuck with him through the ordeal of losing his badge and a year and three months of knocking around until he got the job at the agency. Erica had explained to Tom that she couldn't handle his moods anymore and didn't think she could live with somebody who was stuck in a self-imposed malaise. Tom realized that towards the end their relationship had drifted from being lovers to just roommates. His detachment had become palpable.

He didn't blame her. At times he found himself growing sullen when he dwelled too much on the way things had turned out for him. He wasn't crazy about being a private investigator. It wasn't glamorous work like it was in the old movies or TV shows. It was a lot of spying on people and digging up dirt. The information that he culled often shed light on just how wretched and immoral people could be. Being a cop was different. He saw the same immorality and bad behavior every day, but he could do something about it. Now he just took notes and photographs.

Erica had at one time suggested leaving Buffalo. Maybe they could move down south where Tom could get a job in law enforcement and she could continue her career as an ER nurse. But Tom couldn't leave. Besides the fact that his mother was in town he felt like he had some kind of unfinished business.

Their parting was mostly amicable with Erica saying she loved Tom and would always care about him, but couldn't live with his ghost. Tom had heard from here twice since she moved out. Not that he went out of his way to contact her. Maybe she was right about him. He made a mental note to box up the CDs until he got around to buying a player.

He was tired but restless. He knew he had to do something. He took out his notebook and dialed Gary Shields' private number.

"Who's this?" Shields asked after the second ring.

"Mr. Shields, it's Tom Donovan. I hope I am not disturbing you."

Shields was quiet for a moment as if he had been caught off guard. "Oh, right. Donovan." Another pause. "I was under the impression that I would be dealing with Mr.

Frederickson."

"He had to go downtown to have some records pulled and asked me to call you," Tom lied.

"Well I'm glad to see you guys are moving on this. What can I do for you Mr. Donovan?"

Tom checked his notes. "Mr. Shields, I wanted to ask you about the phone call you received from your wife last night."

Shields thought for a moment. "There wasn't much to it. I tried to reason with her and she told me she wasn't coming back. The whole thing was over in less than five minutes. Like I told you today, I tried to call back several times and eventually got the out of service message."

"Do you remember what time she called?" Tom asked.

"I think it was a little after ten."

"Do you remember hearing any background noise during the call?"

"You think you can find her if I heard some random noise in the background?" Shields asked. The question had a bit of an edge to it.

Now it was Tom's turn to pause and consider what to say next. "We're trying to come up with all the places where she might have gone and looking for any lead," he began. "Anything at all, no matter how minute it might seem at first, could be helpful. So, I know it may seem trivial, but if there was anything you remember?"

Shields exhaled slowly. "Like what?"

"Did it sound like she was indoors or out?"

"Now that you mention it, it did sound like she was standing out in the wind," Shields said.

"Anything else? Traffic noises? Sirens?"

"I think I heard a train."

Now, Tom thought. "Do you think your wife may have called you from the club?"

Shields stopped breathing for a moment and then said, "Why would she be at the club?"

"I don't know, Mr. Shields," Tom responded. "You mentioned she said was tying up loose ends but you didn't mention that Showgirls was in her name."

"Look," Shields said, his voice had tensed slightly. "I didn't think that was relevant and still don't see how it is. To be honest with you the club was in her name because I couldn't get a liquor or entertainment license because of something stupid I did a long time ago."

"Calm down Mr. Shields," Tom said firmly. "I am just trying to make sense of this. If your wife was so opposed to the club then I don't understand why she would sign her name on all the paperwork."

Shields took a second to compose himself. "She was opposed to it from the start. I told her it was a good investment and that I had investors lined up. She went along begrudgingly."

Tom wrote the word 'investors' in his notebook.

That was the first time Shields had mentioned a silent partner or partners. "So what happened to make her sour on the idea?" he asked.

"The few times she went there the more upset she became," Shields said. "I tried to tell her that it was too late to change our minds. As time went along we fought about it more and more"

"I didn't mean to get you upset, but I'm trying to pick up a thread on where your wife may have gone. Part of that is finding out where she was seen last. You're telling me that there is no way she would have called from the club?"

Shields thought it over. "I really doubt it. She hated that place with a passion."

"Alright Mr. Shields. I apologize if this all seems like an invasion of your privacy, but believe me, we just want to locate your wife for you."

"I apologize for being short with you, Donovan. This whole thing is making me crazy."

"Thank you sir, I am sure Mr. Frederickson will be calling you with an update tomorrow. Have a good night."

"Thank you Mr. Donovan."

Tom punched the disconnect button and said out loud, "Goodnight, you lying sack of crap."

Ninety minutes later Tom pulled his car into the side parking lot of Showgirls Gentlemen's Club. He stepped out of his car and looked around. He was starting to feel right about the phone call that Shields got from his wife. The club was in a remodeled boathouse on Dona Avenue. It was one of the few structures remaining on the block. A quarter mile to the west was Lake Erie. There was a stiff breeze coming of the lake just as there could have been last night. As far as the train noise that Shields had heard he could see the rail yard two blocks to the East. He could see why the locals might have resisted. The club was only a few blocks away from one of the oldest neighborhoods in Lackawanna and less than a mile away from a church. But just like the song says Tom thought: Money changes everything.

He approached the front of the building. It bore no resemblance at all to its former self. Tom remembered the place. His grandfather had stored an old wooden Criss Craft there that he claimed had belonged to his great grandfather who used it during Prohibition to run liquor from Canada. As a kid Tom had always wondered why the old man kept it. He never used it.

One of the first things Tom spotted high up on the side wall was a surveillance camera pointed out at the parking lot. It appeared to be stationary but Tom had seen the type before and knew you could use it to pan and zoom in on almost any spot in the lot. As he rounded the corner to the brightly lit front of the building he spotted another camera over the front entrance. He pulled open the tinted glass door and stepped inside.

Tom entered the foyer. To his right there was a counter with a cash register on it. Under the counter's glass top were a bunch of hats, t-shirts and shot glasses with the club's logo on them. Behind the counter sat an oily guy reading a magazine.

Next to a clear glass door that seemed to be vibrating with the sound and light coming from inside the club sat a big Italian looking guy in a black polo shirt looking bored.

The oily guy looked up from his magazine and said, "Ten dollar cover, sport."

Tom put his hands on the counter and looked at the oily guy. "I was wondering if I could talk to the manager."

The Italian looking bouncer stood up. Tom noticed out of the corner of his eye that he was bigger than he thought. The oily guy looked at the bouncer for guidance. Tom turned to look up at him. The guy was easily six foot four with the thick arms and neck of a body builder.

"Ten dollar cover," was all the bouncer said.

"Look, I'm not here for the entertainment," Tom told him. "I just need to talk to the manager," Tom said, trying to be as calm as possible.

The bouncer uncrossed his arms and frowned. "Are you a cop?"

"Why, would I get a discount?" Tom regretted it as soon as he said it.

"Listen, smart ass," the big man said as he pointed a beefy finger at Tom. "Ten bucks or get the fuck out."

Tom started to reach for his coat pocket and the bouncer took a step forward.

"Whoa," Tom said taking a step back. It was no use trying to reason with this Neanderthal. "I'm just going for my wallet." He put his hand inside his coat and took out his wallet.

The giant stepped back and Tom put a ten-dollar bill on the counter. The oily guy rang in the sale and took rubber stamp off of an ink pad to stamp Tom's hand.

"No thanks," Tom said, waiving away the stamp. "But I will need a receipt."

The oily guy looked puzzled for a second and then tore off the receipt paper and handed it to Tom.

After sliding by the bouncer close enough to smell his breath and feel his stare, Tom entered the club. Heavy metal music blasted from the direction of the stage in that ran from the back wall to the middle of the club. The lights on the stage were bright and flashing but everything else seemed to be rather dimly lit. The better to hide stains, Tom thought to himself.

He walked around the outside of the room to the bar that ran along the far wall. After his eyes adjusted he could see the club was about half full. Most of the seats around the stage were empty and about half the tables were occupied. There were five guys at the bar and four of them were looking up at the stage where a very young looking Asian girl had just come out. Tom looked at her and noticed how joyless she looked as she jumped up on the brass pole. There was a tired looking blond behind the bar talking to another patron. Tom was trying to get her attention when he felt a hand on his arm.

"Hi."

Tom turned to see a small thin blond girl with way too much make-up and big silicone enhanced breasts smiling up at him.

"First time here?" she asked, smiling at him.

She was wearing a bikini top and short skirt. Tom's eyes fell to a small rose tattoo over the girls left breast. "Uh yeah," he said looking back up at the girl's face.

"Do you like it?" she asked pointing at the tattoo. "I just had it done." She beamed at Tom. He wondered how old she was under all that make-up.

"It's very nice," he said, looking back down at it briefly. "Did it hurt?"

The girl laughed a little too hard. "Nah, I was pretty buzzed when I had it done." Of course you were, Tom thought. Something over Tom's shoulder caught the girl's eye and she stopped laughing.

"Do you want a table dance?" she asked.

"Not just yet, sweetheart."

The girl looked disappointed and a little desperate.

"I'm just waiting for my buddy to show up. What's

your name, darlin'?" he asked.

"Candy," the girl said trying to smile again.

"As soon as he gets here we'll grab a table and you come find us, okay?"

"Okay," she said and put a finger on Tom's chest. "No backing out now."

"I wouldn't dream of it," he said and smiled.

Candy walked away. Tom watched her approach a table nearby with two young guys who didn't even look like they were old enough to be in the place. They waved her away but not without a good leer.

"Hey Hun, what'll you have?" It was the tired looking barmaid. She had finally made her way down.

Tom threw a twenty on the bar and said, "I'll have a Blue Lite."

He turned away and saw the person who had probably caught Candy's eye during their conversation. Over by the backstage entrance Candy was being lectured by an overweight guy in a black button down shirt that he wore tucked into a very large pair of black jeans. That must be the boss, Tom thought. Candy looked crestfallen. When he was done he turned and headed towards another door that opened onto a staircase. The barmaid brought back eleven dollars and fifty cents. Holy Christ, Tom thought, eight-fifty for a beer. He thought about asking the barmaid for a receipt but dreaded the thought of handing Grace Frederickson a fistful of receipts from a strip club with his expense report.

He left the dollar fifty on the bar and picked up his beer. Tom nonchalantly cased the room to see if there were anymore large angry bouncers to deal with. He leaned on the wall next to door the manager had gone through and swept the room one more time with his eyes. No visible cameras. There was a big rough looking guy with a ponytail on the other side of the stage but his attention was occupied by one of the other dancers.

Tom put his beer down in a large potted plant and ducked through the door.

It was only a half set of stairs in front of him. At the top on the right was a partially opened door. Tom paused at the top of the stairs and took a business card out of his wallet. Over the pounding music coming from the club he heard the faint sound of the man he assumed to be the manager on the phone. He pushed the door open and stuck his head in.

"Hi," he said.

The heavyset man was seated behind a large desk leaning back in his chair, talking on a cell phone. The man looked a little startled.

"Hey," he said into the phone, "I'll call you right back." Then to Tom, "Employees only up here, my friend." Although he didn't sound friendly at all.

Tom snapped his fingers and said, "I'm sorry. I wrote your name down and left my notes in the car."

The man grew agitated. "What the fuck are you talking about? What notes?"

"Ah shit," Tom said grimacing for effect. "My boss didn't call you?"

"I'm gonna ask you one more time. What the fuck are you talking about?"

Tom stepped towards the desk and saw what he wanted. On a table next to the desk was a color monitor with a screen split into six sections. Three of the sections showed camera angles from inside the club. The other three were images from outside the building, including the two cameras Tom had seen. Tom held out his business card.

"Sorry," Tom said. "Gary Shields has hired us to try to find his wife. Somebody from my office should have contacted you."

The man turned the card over in his pudgy fingers and then looked up at Tom. "I heard Gary was looking to hire somebody." He handed the card back to Tom. "I don't see how I can help you."

"Gary told us to leave no stone unturned," Tom said pointing to the monitor. "We understand that Mrs. Shields was here last night and would like to take a look at your surveillance recordings."

"I don't think so," the man said and shook his head.

"Listen," Tom stammered and gestured to the man.

"Frank Cambio." A trickle of sweat appeared on his temple.

"Listen, Frank, Mr. Shields is under the impression that he has to find his wife and soon, before she's in the wind." He pointed to the monitor. "We already know she was here last night and there was an altercation. Whatever else you've got going on is none of our business."

Cambio looked down at his desk and seemed to be thinking.

Time to bluff, Tom decided. "Look," he said pulling out his cell phone. "I can just call Gary Shields on his unlisted number and get this all cleared up."

"Wait a second," Cambio said. He thought for a moment as looked at the phone in Tom's hand. "Let me check it first and then if I think it's okay you can take a look at it." He wiped his brow. "She was here last night. She came when I was out on an errand and let herself into the office. She was here maybe ten minutes tops and then she left. As far as what I heard, she got into it with some drunk in the parking lot and then left."

"What did she want from the office?"

"I think she went into the safe," Cambio replied.

"You don't know for sure? Did you check it?" Tom asked taking out his notebook.

Cambio shook his head. "There are two compartments to the safe. I only have access to the top part for deposits and register money. Only Mr. Shields and Mr. Manzella have the combination for the bottom part."

Tom noticed Cambio tense slightly as he realized

he had let Manzella's name slip. That was noteworthy.

"Mrs. Shields didn't have access to the bottom?" Tom asked.

"Not to my knowledge," Cambio answered. "When Gary called last night he seemed to think that somehow she had got it off of his home computer."

"I see," Tom said. "Frank, I have Mrs. Shields here at about ten-thirty. Is that correct?"

"Yeah, I think so. I got back about eleven and heard all about it."

"Okay," Tom said. "So why don't we just start playback on your machine there at ten-fifteen last night and you can shut it off as soon as we see her leave the parking lot?"

Cambrio frowned.

"Look, Frank," Tom pressed. "We don't want to make any trouble for you or Mr. Shields or Mr Manzella." Bingo, Tom thought. Cambio winced slightly at the mention of Manzella. "I just want to take a look at Donna Shields and see if we can pick up any kind of a trail."

Cambio thought for a moment and then pointed to a chair on the other side of his desk. "Alright, I can do that."

Cambio picked up a remote control and pointed at the box on the shelf underneath the monitor. He entered the search program and punched in the previous days date and the time, ten-fifteen, then he pressed play. The screen flickered and then changed slightly. The images from the front of the building and parking lot showed more garbage being blown around. It had been pretty windy last night.

Tom grew concerned that maybe they had started the playback too late. "Frank, do me a favor and roll back about fifteen minutes."

Cambio protested, "You said ten-fifteen."

"Just fifteen more minutes big guy. I promise that's all"

Cambio reset the machine to playback from 10:00 PM and sure enough at the 10:07 a small white sedan pulled into the west parking lot. A woman resembling Donna Shields got out of the passenger side of the car and headed towards the building. The camera over the front entrance picked her up and then she disappeared into the foyer. A moment later she walked across the barroom and was picked up by the camera at the back of the stage. Tom thought he saw Candy writhing around on the stage floor but couldn't be sure. Donna Shields had gone out of sight.

"Okay she's in. Can you fast forward?" Tom asked.

Cambio picked up the remote and set the playback on 8x speed. Nothing of note happened until the 10:18 mark. Donna Shields walked in front of the stage and Tom said. "Okay, normal speed."

By the time the playback went back to normal speed Donna had already entered the view of the camera on the West lot. It was now visible that she had a bag in her hand that Tom had not noticed when she went in. In her other hand she held what appeared to be a cell phone to her ear for a moment and then closed it. There was also a man a few steps behind her.

"Pause it," Tom said suddenly. Cambio fumbled the remote and then hit pause. Tom reached over the desk and pointed at the screen. "Who is that behind her?"

Cambio stared at the screen for a second and then said, "I have no idea."

Tom could tell he was lying. He let it go. "Okay, can you bring that camera up by itself?"

Cambio hit a button and the west parking lot camera angle now filled up the entire screen.

"Play it," Tom said.

On the screen the man cut off Donna Shields before she reached the car she had arrived in. "Can you zoom in?" Tom asked.

"Yeah but…" Cambio began but didn't finish.

Tom realized what Cambio was going to say. The image had lost some of its resolution and become grainy. As they watched the video the conversation between the man and Donna seemed to be getting rather heated. The man put a hand on the bag Donna was carrying and seemed to be yelling. The man had his back to white sedan and apparently didn't hear the driver's side door open up. A small figure with long dark hair dressed in dark clothes got out and very quickly and very deliberately walked up behind the man and stuck something onto the side of his neck. The man's body went rigid and then crumpled to the ground.

"Holy shit," Tom said before he could stop himself. The recording played on and Donna and her passenger got into the car and drove away.

Cambio paused the recording. He turned to Tom but didn't say anything.

"Sorry," Tom said, regaining his composure and returning to his notebook. "So you have no idea who the guy is we just saw get tazed?"

"None," Cambio said.

"How about the person that tazed him? Don't suppose you know her?"

"I just assumed it was just some bitch friend of Donna's," Cambio said with a little venom.

"Okay, so what happed to the guy lying out in your parking lot? Let's see what happens to him."

"He just got up a few minutes and walked away," Cambio said. "Went out of the camera range and just left."

"Any idea who called the police?" Tom asked.

"No."

"Okay." Tom would have really liked to see if that was true but didn't want to push is luck. "Can you burn me a DVD of the segment you showed me?"

"What for?" Tom asked.

"I can have it enhanced and try to get an ID on

Donna's friend maybe get an ID on the car."

Cambio sat breathing heavily. He was turning something over in his mind.

"Frank, if you are worried about your mystery man I could give a rat's ass about him. You and I could dick around here for the next week while Donna slips out of town with her friend."

Cambio narrowed his eyes. "Alright, give me a minute," he said. "Go wait downstairs and I'll burn a copy."

Tom went downstairs and looked in the potted plant. The bottle was gone. He would have felt odd retrieving it anyway so he just leaned on the wall by the doorway.

Candy came up to him looked up and smiled. "Did your friend stiff you?" she asked.

"Yeah he did," Tom said smiling again. "The prick just called me, said his wife flipped out when she found out. Can you believe that?"

"I guess so," Candy laughed. "Is your wife okay with you being in a place like this?"

"I'm not married," Tom said and felt himself blush.

"Bullshit," Candy said still smiling. "A good looking guy like you?"

She stepped closer and put a hand on Tom's arm. He could smell perfume and sweat. The top of her head came up to his shoulder and when she looked up at him he noticed that her pupils were slightly dilated. He had a sudden attack of conscience.

"So, how much is a table dance?" he asked.

Candy brightened a little. "Twenty for a regular, fifty for a private dance in the VIP room."

Tom looked back at the doorway up to the office and then took out his wallet. He took out a twenty-dollar bill and the business card that Cambio had given back to him. He looked Candy straight in the eye and handed them to her.

"Listen, sweetheart, I've got a confession to make," he started. "I was really here to see your boss about Donna Shields."

Candy looked confused. Tom continued, "Her husband hired me to try to find her and I didn't want to say anything about it before I had a chance to talk to Frank. It's kind of hard to explain. I will take that dance some other time but in the meantime if there is anything that you may know about Donna or Gary Shields my number is on that card. Call it anytime."

Candy took the twenty and the card. She looked at it and Tom wondered if she thought it was just some cheap pickup ploy. Suddenly she got nervous.

"Look you don't have to give me any money," she told him.

"Keep it," Tom cut her off. "Frank will be down here in an second and I don't want you to get in trouble." He checked around to see if they were being watched. It didn't appear so and from what he remembered the spot he was standing in wasn't covered by the camera over the stage.

"I don't know," Candy said. She seemed truly upset now.

"Hey, hey, don't worry about it," Tom replied. "If it makes you nervous just throw the card out and keep the twenty. Like I said, the last thing I want is to get you into a jam."

Candy looked up and smiled faintly. "Okay." She put the twenty and the card into the small purse she was carrying. Just then Frank Cambio came down the stairs. To her credit, Candy was able to snap back into character. She put her hand on Tom's cheek and said, "Okay, maybe next time handsome." She turned and was gone.

Cambio handed Tom a DVD in a plain white paper sleeve. "Here you go," he said. "Remember, you promised to use only what you need."

"My word is gold Frankie," Tom said, putting the disc into his coat pocket. "Thanks."

Cambio frowned. "So you got what you need?"

"Yep."

"So you'll be leaving?"

"Sure, Frank," Tom said and grinned. "Like I said I could give a rat's ass what goes on here. If it's okay with Mr. Shields I don't care if you guys are having pagan sacrifices right on stage."

Cambio frowned again. His phone must of vibrated

because he fished it out of his pocket looked at the caller ID and with one last dirty look at Tom he turned to go back up the stairs as he opened his phone.

Tom made his way around the stage and towards the foyer. As he opened the door he looked over his shoulder and saw the rough looking guy he had pegged as another bouncer talking to a balding guy in his mid forties. I'll be damned if the balding guy doesn't' look like the guy who got zapped last night, Tom thought.

"Time to go," said a voice as Tom felt a hand on his shoulder. The big doorman started pushing Tom through the foyer past the counter.

"I just saw an old friend of mine," Tom said. The phone behind the counter rang and the oily cashier picked it up.

"Well, you can catch up with him some other time," the giant said putting a hand Tom's chest. Tom was being pushed back through the main doorway now.

"Is this because I didn't get my hand stamped?" Tom asked.

From behind the doorman the cashier said urgently, "Larry that was Frank. He said to get the disc back from this guy and then get him out of here."

"Larry?" Tom asked while that sank in with the doorman. "I had you pegged for a Vince or a Rocco."

Larry the doorman smirked and with his left hand still on Tom's chest he pushed him the rest of the way outside. "Let's have that disc smart ass."

Tom took a step back onto the sidewalk and said, "Nah, I don't think so."

Without a word Larry bull rushed Tom to try to grab him. Tom had already decided that it would probably be best to stay out of this guys reach. The doorman was ten years younger, six inches taller and probably fifty pounds heavier. With one move Tom deflected the big man's grasp and moved off on an angle. He then brought his knee up, driving it into Larry's thigh.

Larry clutched his thigh for a second and then uncoiled from that position with a round-house left. Tom's boxing instincts had already kicked in. He ducked the blow and as his opponent's momentum carried him forward came up with a right hand into the ribs. Larry expelled a loud breath but he wasn't done. He straightened up to resume his attack but before he could Tom hit him with a left to the jaw and then, as Larry stood dazed, put all of his weight into a right hand to the bridge of Larry's nose. The pop of the cartilage was audible over the music coming out of the club. Larry teetered for a second and then fell backwards onto his rear end.

Tom heard the door open and turned to see the oily cashier pointing a silver hand gun at him. "Hold it right there asshole," he yelled.

Tom took a step back and put his hands up slightly. "He fell."

"Shut the fuck up and stay right there," the cashier said.

Just then the other man Tom had pegged for a bouncer came out through the foyer. He had graying hair pulled back in a pony-tail and a goatee. He stepped passed the cashier and looked at Larry then at Tom. "Boy," he said to Tom. "That was fucking stupid."

Chapter 7

The bouncer took a step towards Tom, who now realized that his right hand was starting to hurt like hell. Larry the doorman was starting to come to his senses and wiped his bleeding nose into his hand. "Motherfucker," he said.

Then a short blare of a siren and the flash of red and blue lights. Tom heard the sound of tires pull up behind him.

He turned around to see a black and white SUV marked with *Lackawana Police* on the side and in smaller print on the fender it said *Patrol Supervisor*. The lights were turned off and a tall stocky man with silver hair visible under his black cap got out and assessed the situation. Tom thought to himself that he pretty nonchalant considering the situation. He looked over his shoulder at the cashier and the gun he had held a moment ago was out of sight. Larry had risen to his feet and everyone else stood where they were.

Tom looked back at the cop. The name badge on his jacket said Lt. Kruger.

"What's up fellahs?" Kruger asked.

"This guy was making a nuisance of himself so

Larry told him to leave," the cashier said. "He took a swing at Larry."

Just then Cambio, the manager, came out through the door. He looked at Kruger and then at Larry and frowned.

Kruger looked at Cambio and said with false cordiality, "Oh, hi Frank. What kind of bullshit are you boys getting into tonight?"

Cambio's face flushed despite the chill in the air. He pointed at Tom and said, "That guy stole something from me."

"That's not what Marty said," Kruger said and he pointed at the cashier. "He said he was creating a nuisance inside and then Larry was in the process of throwing him out when he apparently got his ass kicked."

Tom glanced at Larry who was steaming mad. He was sure if the cop hadn't been there it would have been on to round two.

No one said anything for a moment and then Kruger walked up to Tom and said, "What's your name, son?"

"Tom Donovan."

Kruger thought for a second and then the flicker of recognition. "The Donovan from Buffalo PD?"

"Formerly," Tom answered.

"Right." Kruger scratched his chin. He looked over at Cambio and then back at Tom. "Well Tom Donovan, were you creating a disturbance here or did you remove property from the club?"

Tom thought about lying but then figured he should play it straight. "In my coat pocket I have a DVD that Cambio gave me. Believe it or not I am working for his boss, Gary Shields, trying to locate his wife. There was some confusion when I was leaving and then this guy," he pointed at Larry, "over-reacted and I was forced to defend myself."

"Bullshit!" Larry yelled taking his bloody hand away from his face.

Kruger turned on Larry and held up an index finger sternly. He looked back at Tom.

"Kind of looks like you assaulted him." He jerked his thumb towards Larry.

"Take a look at their security cameras," Tom said. "He put his hands on me first."

"And what is on that DVD that seems to have started this whole thing?" Kruger asked.

Tom responded, "A surveillance recording of Mrs. Shields and an associate leaving the club in a white sedan. I think the identity of the associate might give us a lead on Mrs. Shields whereabouts. Mr. Cambio gave it to me."

Kruger remained standing in front of Tom but turned to face Cambio. "I thought you said he stole it Frankie?"

Cambio was at a loss for a moment. Then he said, "Well, half of his story is bullshit."

Tom sat back and let Kruger work. "Which half

would that be?" Kruger asked.

"It's true he's working for Mr. Shields, but he had no business poking around the club," Cambio said nervously.

Kruger thought for a moment then said, "So why did you give him the disc?"

Cambio became indignant. "He tricked me."

Kruger frowned. "As much as I believe that wouldn't be that hard to do," he started, "something about this isn't making sense."

Cambio sputtered, "What are you saying?"

Kruger continued, "Well we could all go to the station and have Mr. Shields come down to clear all this up." He looked at the club's employees one by one. "I'm sure he would love another call from us at this hour."

"So this guy comes here and misrepresents himself then assaults one of my employees and that's it?" Cambio said, almost pleading. He was running out of steam.

Kruger stepped to the middle of the sidewalk and looked directly at Cambio silencing him. "Let's just call this a misunderstanding. You boys get back inside and I'll see that Mr. Donovan here leaves the premises."

Cambio started to protest but thought better of it. He opened the club door and gestured for the other three employees to get inside.

"Oh and Frankie," Kruger said getting Cambio's attention. "We have already had several conversations about keeping your bullshit inside the club and off my street."

Cambio's mouth tightened into a grimace and then he disappeared inside.

Kruger turned back to Tom and raised his eyebrows.

"Uh, so I should go then?" Tom asked.

"Not just yet," Kruger told him. He pointed towards the SUV. "Hop in. We should have a little talk." He stepped over to the curb and opened the back door.

Kruger didn't speak while he backed up and pulled into the parking lot. "Which one is yours?" he said gesturing out the windshield.

"It's the Gray Chevy straight ahead," Tom answered.

Kruger pulled in front of Tom's car and adjusted the mirror so he could see Tom in the back seat. "Shame about what happened at the projects," he said and shook his head slightly. "It sounded like you got screwed over but good for doing your job."

Tom always hated when it came up, but by now he was getting used to it. "Not as bad as my partner did," he answered.

Kruger looked out ahead and said, "Yeah that's a rough way to retire." Then he looked back in the mirror at Tom. "That bouncer is a big one. Not real bright but still, how'd you get over on him?"

"I used to box when I was younger."

Kruger had another realization. "Fast Tommy Donovan?"

Tom blushed slightly, he hadn't heard the nickname

in a while. "Yeah, you must really be an enthusiast to remember that."

"Oh I fought a little and trained a couple of guys when I was younger," Kruger said. "You made quite a splash in the Gold Gloves. What was it? 1991?"

"'93," Tom replied. "Then I got taken apart by Ramirez."

Kruger smiled and shook his head. "I remember him. He turned pro, didn't he?"

"Yeah, he had a couple of fights but had to quit due to concussions." Tom was getting antsy. "Look, Lieutenant, Not that I mind talking about the old days but was there something else you wanted to say?"

Kruger chuckled. "Yeah." He paused for a second. "As a personal favor I'd like to ask you to steer clear of this place. We have been keeping an eye on it since it opened and I don't have to tell you it brings all kinds of assholes out of the woodwork."

"Uh, thanks," Tom said.

Kruger smiled and said, "Not you specifically, Donovan. All I'm saying is the less bullshit we have to deal with down here the better."

"Understood," Tom said. "Trust me, this was a one time thing."

"Fair enough," Kruger said. He got out of the SUV and opened Tom's door.

Tom got out and shook Kruger's extended hand.

"Sure wish I could have seen you take down that big Dago."

Tom smiled wanly and shrugged. "Lucky shot."

"Bullshit," Kruger said. He fake cocked his right fist. "Not for 'Fast Tommy' Donovan." He got back into the SUV and drove off.

Later at Tom's apartment he cracked a beer and thought about turning on the TV but the thought didn't excite him at all. The adrenaline was finally wearing off and he was exhausted. He ate a sandwich and drained the beer. Getting ready for bed he turned the day's events over in his mind. Trent. That piece of shit was reaching out to him from the grave. He wasn't concerned about himself so much, he had already lost much of what he had and what he was. But to make Joe Walczak and his mother and everyone else go through it all again was tying his stomach in knots.

Then there was Donna Shields. The more he found out about her husband the less he felt like helping him find her. He found himself passing judgments again and knew what Cal would say about that. He had a job to do now. He had to keep busy while the civil suit played itself out. He had to keep his head above water.

CHAPTER 8

Tom awoke at 5:45 AM, unable to sleep with such a restless mind. He had over three hours to kill before he was supposed to meet his grandfather. He pulled on his trainers and headed out for a run. At the end of his three-mile course he reluctantly picked up a copy of the News and headed back to his apartment.

The story about the lawsuit was on the front page below the fold. A pretty neutral piece, Tom thought as he read it. Reverend Mason was quoted briefly, but his words didn't seem to have the same fire in print as they did live or on television. A hearing would be scheduled as soon as counsel filed the requisite paperwork. He thought about calling Joe, but it was early and he wouldn't know how to start. He felt almost as bad as he had felt two years before. As soon as he had been released from custody after the shooting after he went to see Joe at the hospital only to find he was still in surgery and Joe's wife Lisa inconsolable. Tom remembered the way Lisa had looked at him. Was it his own guilt or was she saying something with her eyes?

Tom took a shower and stood in front of the mirror to shave. He noticed the dark circles under his eyes and the flecks of gray hair starting to show at his temples. He had put on twenty pounds since his boxing days but none of it was fat. He went to the kitchen, made a pot of coffee and tried to read the rest of the paper.

At 8:45 Tom pulled up in front of Donovan's Tavern on South Park Avenue. The cool damp of the previous evening was gone and the sun was shining. It looked like spring had finally arrived.

His grandfather's bar stood about a quarter mile from the brown-field that used to be the Republic Steel plant. The city had purchased the land after the plant was razed and every few years some developer would unveil plans for new homes or a business park, but so far nothing. Tom thought it would be a long time before somebody actually thought it was smart, or safe for that matter, to build on the grounds of a defunct steel plant.

Back in the day Donovan's was one of many bars that thrived in the neighborhood. The steel plant was bustling twenty four hours a day and the neighborhood was flush with blue collar men who made the taverns the social centers of South Buffalo. Checks were cashed at the bars, lunch was served, fights were fought and life went on.

Hugh Donovan was a visionary. He seemed to know as early as the mid-sixties that the steel boom wasn't going to last forever and when the plants went away so would all the bars and mom and pop grocery stores that dotted the community. Hugh's own father had dabbled in questionable activities during the Depression and Hugh realized that he may need to diversify in that direction a bit to keep the family business afloat.

So he started making book out of the bar's back room. At first a little number running and then some sporting events. When his business got big enough, he evicted his upstairs tenant and moved his operation to the apartment over the bar. At its height there were four phones, three televisions wired to the bars satellite dish and a teletype machine that got feeds from the major wire services. Hugh also recognized that it could be a rough business. So in response to the welchers and the con men and the Italians on the West side he assembled a cadre of tough, thick-necked guys, mostly as a deterrent, but occasionally as the deliverers of justice according to Hugh Donovan's law. Hugh also encouraged his employees to make money however they saw fit, as long as it wasn't drugs or whores. Those things violated his principles. Over time he became feared and loved at the same time, sort of an iron fisted Robin Hood. He helped keep the neighborhood safe and his friends never went without. But God help you if you crossed him

Over time though, the bookmaking business became a dinosaur. First the State of New York muscled in with the lottery and off track betting. He had survived two raids by the state police (some of the local cops were his best customers) on his operation. then the state wised up and got in on the action. Then the Indians and the internet made it too easy for people to gamble. That and the fact that many of his old customers had either died off or just dried up and left town like the steel companies they worked for.

So Hugh kept the bar going and looked out over what remained of his fiefdom. No one except Hugh and maybe one or two of his inner circle knew exactly what the old man was worth or how much he still had coming in. He claimed he was retired but Tom had his doubts.

Tom entered the bar's front door and his waited for his eyes to adjust to the dark. The place reeked of beer and cigarette smoke, which was odd due to the fact that the state had banned smoking in public places a few years back.

"Hiya handsome." It was Bonnie, the bleach blond, sixty-something bartender who had worked there for what seemed like forever. There were two old guys at the bar who looked up at Tom briefly and they turned back to their beer glasses.

"Bonnie, how do you do it?" Tom asked her.

Bonnie cocked her head suspiciously. "Do what?"

"Work in a place like this and get prettier every time I see you?"

Bonnie smiled and said, "Ah, you're such a bullshitter. But that's why I love you. We don't see you enough Tommy. You look so thin. You need a good woman in your life."

"Are you volunteering?" Tom asked with a smile.

Bonnie laughed her smoker's laugh. "Ha, I'm old

enough to be your mother's much younger sister."

Tom smiled wider. "Is the old man in?"

"Yep, he's in the back. Go on in."

Tom walked into the back room. There were two men seated at one of the three tables, his grandfather Hugh Donovan and Robert Stanley, the attorney who had represented him at his shooting trial.

Tom had not seen Hugh in almost two years. He noticed that the old man looked every one of his eighty-six years. In fact it looked like he had lost weight since the last time Tom had seen him. The graying skin on his face hung loosely, but the eyes were still bright and sharp.

Bob Stanley was dressed in a well-made dark suit that had the look of being expensive without being flashy. His thinning gray hair was cropped close to his scalp and he had his usual calm but alert demeanor. Bob Stanley was one of the last people he expected to see at Donovan's Tavern at 9:00 AM on a Tuesday morning.

Stanley broke the silence. He stood up and extended his hand. "Tom, it's good to see you. How have you been?"

Tom shook Stanley's hand while he tried to make sense of things. He looked from Stanley to his grandfather. Their eyes met and locked for a moment.

"Have a seat kid," the old man finally said. "Coffee?"

"No, I'm good," Tom responded sitting down across from Hugh. Stanley returned to his seat on Tom's right. "Whitey said you wanted to see me."

Hugh smirked. "I'm fine. How are you?" He was still staring into Tom's eyes.

"Sorry," Tom said, "I guess I shouldn't be so rude. Good to see you granddad." There was a trace of sarcasm in his voice.

Stanley decided to try to cut the tension. "Tom before you get worked up about me being here, I should tell you that this was my idea."

Tom turned to Stanley. "What was your idea?"

"Well I wanted to contact you yesterday but I realized I didn't have your number. I called your office but they said you were out," Stanley said then he hesitated. "I called your grandfather and asked if he knew how to get a hold of you and he set this up." Stanley gestured with his hands at the table.

Tom shook his head and said, "I appreciate your concern Mr. Stanley, and I do appreciate you keeping me out of prison the last time, but I think your services might be a little out of my price range."

Stanley looked like he was about to say something but Tom kept going, "I live in a crappy little apartment, I have an eight year old car with one hundred thousand miles on it and about a grand in the bank."

Hugh chimed in, "And I would offer to help but the little son of a bitch is too proud to take it."

Tom turned to the old man and said, "Help like that

I don't need."

Hugh shook his head again and chuckled. "I'm your father's father boy. I'm your family, not the devil."

Tom held his tongue at that.

Stanley took over again. "Tom look, the next couple of days are going to be important. Do you have a lawyer?"

"Not yet," Tom said.

"At least let me do the written response to the suit. If you find somebody else, fine. I would still like to act as a consultant on a pro-bono basis."

Tom thought about that as he studied Stanley. "Not to sound ungrateful, but why would you do that?"

Now Stanley smiled. "Tom, I know what cops and ex-cops think of lawyers and a lot of it's true. What happened to you two years ago was wrong and now Mason has manipulated Trent's mother into this lawsuit. I believe it's all part of his master plan to run for a seat on the common council on the next ballot. It was wrong two years ago and it's even more wrong now for him to use it for political gain."

"God help us," Hugh said.

Tom thought for a second. The price was right and Stanley was an excellent attorney. Still there must be a catch. "I should probably talk to Joe Walczak."

"He already has representation," Stanley said.

"What? Who?" Tom stammered.

"He retained some big shot from Albany, Sheldon

Sumner. I spoke to Joe's wife yesterday. Made the same offer and she said 'Thanks, but no thanks.'"

Tom was a little stunned. Joe had sure reacted quickly and without even talking to him. He had to talk to Joe. He finally relented. If there was a catch to Stanley's offer he would deal with it later. The fact that Stanley was already familiar with the case and willing at least to start working on his behalf made him feel slightly better. "Okay Bob, I really appreciate it."

"Great," Stanley said and stood up. "Now if you will excuse me I have to be downtown by ten. I can have a letter drafted and sent to Judge Meyers by this afternoon."

"What's the letter for?" Tom asked.

"In a civil case the defendant's first step is to send a written response to the court, in this case Judge Meyers, responding to the allegations. Of course, by responding I mean denying. After that it's the discovery phase. And I already have a few ideas on that if you decide you want me to do it."

Tom stood up and shook Stanley's hand and took his business card. "Call me this afternoon if you get a chance Tom."

"I will. And thanks again, Bob."

Stanley turned to Hugh and shook his hand. "Good to see you again Hugh."

"Same here, counselor," Hugh said. Tom noticed that Hugh's hand was shaking.

Tom let Stanley get out of earshot and looked at his grandfather. He remained standing. "You sure you had nothing to do with this?" Tom asked.

"Like I said, I knew you wouldn't like it if you thought I was interfering," his grandfather responded.

"It's complicated."

Hugh smiled, somewhat sadly. "Not really Tommy. I know there is a part of you that will always blame me for what happened to your dad but God knows I had nothing to do with it."

Tom looked back, trying to look impassive. He looked over Hugh's head at the framed photos hanging over on the paneled wall. There was a picture of himself at eighteen in the ring with Johnson. Next to that was a picture of his father in his boxing gear, holding up a trophy. The caption under the picture said "1970 Gold Gloves light heavyweight Champion Tom Donovan." Next to that was a picture of Hugh shaking hands with the late former mayor at what looked like the St. Patrick's Day Parade.

Hugh noticed Tom was looking at the photos. "In a lot of ways you're very much like your father," Hugh said. "You can be as stubborn as a mule and hold a grudge like an old washer woman." Hugh looked down into his coffee cup. "It's up to you what you choose to believe or not believe Tommy."

Suddenly the old man seemed pitiable. The sensation made Tom uncomfortable. Years ago Hugh had accused Tom's Uncle Sam of turning Tom against him. He had assured his grandfather over time that that was not the case, that it was Hugh's lifestyle and avocation, the same lifestyle and that Tom believed his father had been caught up in that he found intolerable.

"Look, I'll stop by again and we can have a beer," Tom said

"You can have a beer. I can't. God damned diabetes."

"Okay, but I have to get to the office."

Hugh looked up again and said, "Okay kid, but one more thing."

"What's that?"

"That strip bar you were at last night," Hugh began.

Tom was taken aback but not shocked. Whitey Brennan had been right; the old man was still all-seeing.

"What about it?" Tom asked.

"Be careful around those people, they can be real bastards."

Tom didn't have time to ask what the old man meant or how he even knew about his trip to the club. "It was a one time visit Hugh. Not my kind of place." His phoned buzzed in his pocket. "I gotta go."

"Okay, go on." Hugh waved him away.

Tom dug the phone out of his jacket and answered it on the fourth ring. It was Grace. "Tom, where are you?" she asked.

"I had to make a personal call, a little family business," Tom responded.

He waved to Bonnie as he walked by the bar, she winked at him as she drew a beer.

"You better get in here ASAP," Grace said. "Cal wants to see you before you do anything else."

That was seldom a good thing Tom thought as he pushed his way out into the sunlight.

"I'm on my way."

Grace clicked off without saying goodbye.

Chapter 9

Tom jumped on the Skyway and drove downtown. The morning traffic was starting to ebb so he made it to the office in twenty minutes. As he pushed open the outer door in to the reception area Grace looked up and started to speak. Tom saw the door to Cal's office was closed and quickly put his index finger up to his lips. Grace scowled at him and crossed her arms in front of her.

Tom mouthed the words, "One minute," to her. Grace shook her head but didn't say anything. He nodded to her and went quietly down the hall to Brian's office.

Brian was sitting at his desk staring intently at his computer monitor. He had ear buds in but Tom could hear the muffled sound of heavy metal music just the same. It took him several seconds to get Brian's attention. Brian killed the music and took the headphones out.

"Major Tom. What's up?" Brian asked.

"You're in early," Tom replied.

"Never went home," Brian told him. Tom noticed then that Brian was in the same sweatshirt and jeans he had on yesterday and his office had a very stale scent to it.

"Wow, that's dedication."

"Well, the better you guys do the better I do."

"How is that?" Tom asked.

Brian rocked back in his chair. "Well, the boss may act like a dinosaur but he's a pretty savvy business man."

Tom smirked and said, "I've heard him called a lot of things but never that."

"No, no, he is a forward thinker," Brian said in all seriousness. "He is all about incentives and productivity. Every check the firm brings in the Bri-meister gets a percentage. Between you Travis and Sherry I had enough work to fuel and all-nighter."

"Hmm, I didn't know that about him," Tom said, faking interest. "I guess I am on his screaming and yelling incentive plan."

Brian thought for a second and said, "You need to learn how to negotiate better." He picked up a sheaf of papers from the corner of his desk. "Here is some stuff I printed out for you."

Tom took the papers. "What is it?"

"Some more information on the principles involved in the Shields thing. A lot of it seemed pretty trivial, but I thought I'd let you sort that out."

Tom heard Cal's voice down the hall. He had to hurry. He took the DVD Cambio had given him the night before and held it up. "Can you do anything with this surveillance video?" he asked Brian.

"Like what?"

"Get some stills. There are two women and a man getting into a scrape in a parking lot. I already know that one of the women is Donna Shields." Tom lowered his voice as he heard Cal storm down the hall towards his and Sherry's office. "I want to try to identify the other woman and the man and maybe get a plate number off the white sedan the women leave in."

They heard Cal's voice again now at the other end of the hall.

Brian took the disc. "I have better software for that at home. I could take a look at it when I go to lunch."

"That would be great."

The door flew open then and Tom turned to see Cal glaring at him.

"Oh," Brian said.

Cal pointed at Tom and said quietly, "Come with me." Then he turned to Brian. "You and I will talk later."

Cal spent the next ten minutes with Tom in his office, with the door closed, yelling about how he couldn't understand how Tom had survived ten years as a policeman if he couldn't comprehend and follow a few simple instructions. He went on to point out that Gary Shields was very upset that Tom was going around punching out his employees and poking around in things that had nothing to do with finding his wife. He also stated that he received a call from a Lt. Kruger from the Lackawana PD. Kruger had termed it a 'courtesy' call but Cal said there was more than a little bit of menace behind it. Finally he sat down and lit his dormant cigar.

"Alright, your turn," Cal said nodding towards Tom. "Explain what the hell you were doing last night."

Tom exhaled and began, "First of all Shields lied."

"Shields lied about what?" Cal asked.

"His wife owns the club. On paper anyway."

"What does that have to do with anything?"

"She called him," Tom said. "The night before last from the club after she took something out of the safe."

"Again, I ask you, what does that have to do with it?" Cal asked, growing more irritated.

Tom was starting to wonder if he was going to get fired this very afternoon. "I think she's running from him."

That seemed to get Cal's attention. "And why would you say that?"

"Whatever she took from the safe was important enough for some guy to follow her out of the bar to try and get it back by force. Then a little friend of hers pops out of the shadows and tazes the guy. I think Shields may be mixed up in something beyond the realm of adult entertainment."

Cal sat back and took a draw on his cigar. "That's a pretty big leap from point A to point B. Do you have anything else?"

"The silent partner Shields forgot to tell us about," Tom said.

Now Cal's interest was piqued. "Who would that

be?"

Tom took out his notebook and turned a couple of pages. "Somebody named Manzella."

Cal put his cigar in the ashtray on the slide out shelf on his desk. "Did you get a first name?"

"Not yet."

Cal turned to his computer. He typed in a few things and then sat back in his chair. "Was this guy Manzella at the club?" Cal asked as he scrolled down his screen.

"I wouldn't know if he was or not," Tom said. "The name sounds kind of familiar but I couldn't place it. So I wouldn't know him if he was standing right in front of me."

Cal turned his computer monitor around so Tom could see it. "Now this is just a hunch," Cal began, "but did you see anybody that looked like this?"

Tom looked at the screen. There was a picture of a gruff looking man from a mug shot. On the corner of the photo was the inscription BPD 10/24/2004. He had little doubt.

"Holy shit," Tom said. "Yeah I saw him twice. The first time was on the surveillance video getting zapped and the second time I saw him standing at the bar as I was being shoved out. Who is he?"

Cal turned the monitor back and frowned at it. "Michael Manzella. He and I have a little history."

"What history?" Tom asked.

"He was one of the last cases that I worked when

I was in Homicide," Cal told him. "We popped him for killing a drug dealer in Black Rock, but he got off when our eye witness recanted. The Fed's grabbed him a year later though. He was sent upstate on a drug rap." Cal scratched his chin and thought. "I didn't think he would be out so soon."

Cal went silent and seemed to be lost in thought. Tom interrupted.

"Yeah, but who is he and what would he have to do with Gary Shields?" Tom asked.

"Back in the late 70's and early 80s the FBI dismantled most of the mob in Buffalo," Cal said as he looked out his window. "Most of the guys who didn't go to jail either went straight or went underground or a little bit of both. Mike Manzella's father went to Federal prison on a RICO beef. He died of lung cancer in '85. That doesn't mean Mike is connected or anything, but I wouldn't rule out the fact that he may be part of some kind of new organization. Not to stereotype, but a strip club would be a nice place to launder money among other things." Cal seemed to drift off as he finished.

"Okay, so now what do we do?"

Cal picked up the cigar and looked at it then said, "We continue to look for Donna Shields." He looked at Tom. "But you stay away from the club and if you have any questions for Mr. Shields you let me ask them."

"What about Manzella and the club? Are we just

going to pretend they don't exist?"

Cal glared at Tom. "Did you hear me say anything like that? One thing you have to learn Tom is to not assume you know what's going through another man's mind."

Tom felt himself blushing slightly. He didn't know what to say.

Cal softened up slightly. "Just get out there and find Donna Shields and don't even think of doing anything stupid like last night without running it past me."

Tom stood up. "Got it."

Tom stuck his head in Brian's office on his way down to his own only to find Brian had left already. Tom hoped that Brian was indeed going home to look at the DVD he had given him. Brian's lunch breaks could last anywhere from a half hour to two days. Tom looked at the printouts Brian had given him and decided to check them out.

Sherry was at her desk when Tom came in working on an expense report. She glanced up at him and said, "I take it Cal found you?"

"Oh yeah," Tom replied.

He sat down with his back to Sherry and started in on the intel that Brian had culled. He heard Sherry slide her chair back and stand up.

"So, what's that place like?" she asked.

"Cal's office? It's pretty depressing."

"No, smart ass. I meant Showgirls?"

Tom turned to face her. He tried to read her

expression but couldn't.

"Pretty typical strip club," he told her. "Brass poles, leather seats, overpriced drinks."

"Let me ask you then, what does a guy get out of a place like that?"

If Sherry would have been a man, or even another cop, Tom may had said something off color.

"Hell Sherry, I'm no psychologist."

"What do you get out of it?" she asked

Tom thought for a second and looked down. He was taken aback by the line of questioning. He looked at Sherry and tried to figure out where this was headed. He had always tried to treat her as an equal first, but there was no denying she was attractive. He wondered if that made him subconsciously treat her differently than if she were one of the overweight retired cops who worked down the hall.

"Not too much since I was about twenty one," he said and then paused. "Actually, if you ask me, they're pretty depressing places. A bunch of grim, desperate guys getting fleeced by a bunch of girls with daddy issues."

He looked up and noticed Sherry was frowning. She un-furrowed her brow and said, "That sounds like a pretty sound psychological assessment from a layman."

"Nah, just a veteran of being a male in the twenty first century. Are you all done with the Burroughs thing?" He could feel himself blushing slightly and needed to change the subject.

She held up the expense report and said, “Yep. I’m going to take couple of days off. Get caught up on some stuff around the apartment.” She started to leave than turned back around. “Oh and the offer still stands Tom, if you need any help with the Trent thing let me know.”

“Thanks Sherry.” And she was gone.

Tom dug into the stack of papers in front of him. There was detailed information on both Gary and Donna Shields a lot of information on Gary’s business dealings, both past and present. There was information on Gary’s meteoric career as a financial planner. In the span of a few short years he went from a smiling, confident up and comer to a pariah. Then his foray into real estate. Not a lot of information about this enterprise. It looked like another guy who made a killing flipping houses and got out before the housing market went south. Brian had included a few clippings of property liens and fines from different housing agencies, but for the most part Shields seemed to have cleaned all of them up.

And then the leap into commercial realty. It looked like Shields had entered the market with guns blazing, buying up existing storefronts and strip malls and brokering deals for new properties. Brian must have noticed the same thing because he had made a note in the margin that said, ‘How many houses did this guy flip to come up with this kind of bankroll?’ Good question, Tom thought. He decided to put Gary Shields aside and look at Donna.

Most of the information in Donna's file Brian had already told him. He appeared to be a good kid, good student, scholarship to the University of Rochester Business School. Graduated in '99 and worked at the downtown office of an international bank until shortly after she got married.

The information about her family was something else altogether. The article about the disappearance of Donna's stepfather, David Stanton, said he was retired car dealer who ran a small but successful lot out in Williamsville. What struck Tom as odd was that the same clipping gave Stanton's age at the time of his disappearance as fifty-two years old. That seemed a little young to Tom for a guy to shutter a profitable business, pull up stakes and leave town without a trace unless there were some extenuating circumstances.

Then he was on to Donna's half-sister Angela Cryer. Angela had been arrested when she was 17 on a drug charge. It was bad enough that she was being charged as an adult. In a press clipping Brian had included the DA had alluded to the fact that Angela had been in trouble before. The case was dismissed and it was agreed that if Angela stayed out of trouble she would be allowed to live under her sister's supervision. That seemed to do the trick because that was the last mention of Angela Stanton from the police and court section. Three years later she had graduated from the local community college with a certificate in dental hygiene. Two years after that she was married to a guy named Robert Cryer and then a year later a birth announcement for a daughter Leyla Donnatella Cryer. In six short years she seemed to have transformed from juvenile delinquent to working suburban mom.

There were ten more pages of information from Brian. Tom read through them but nothing jumped out at him. He sat back in his chair and thought about what to do next.

His mind came back to the half-sister, Angela. Shields had said that he had spoken to her and that Donna had not contacted her. Then again Shields had already omitted or obfuscated a couple of key facts so what did that mean? He picked up the sheet with the information on Angela Cryer and looked up her work number. He reached over and pushed his office door shut and then picked up the phone. He dialed the number and it was picked up on the third ring.

"Good morning, Harris Hill Dental, this is Gina. How can I help you?"

"I was wondering if I could speak to Angela Cryer?" Tom asked.

"Would you like to schedule an appointment?"

"Uh, no actually I am calling for the Erie Community College Alumni Association," Tom said. "We're contacting recent graduates for a survey. It's nothing urgent."

"Oh, actually Angela called in today."

"Okay, no big deal. I'll try her at home. Thank you."

"Have a nice day."

"You too, Gina." He hung up.

He looked down the page and saw Angela's home phone number. He put his hand back on the phone, but then had a thought. Brian had also included Angela's home address. It was too easy for somebody to hang up the phone on you. Tom grabbed his coat and headed for the door.

Chapter 10

Tom grabbed one of the GPS devices out of the storage cabinet in Brian's office and headed out to his car. He plugged it in and punched in Angela Cryer's address in Clarence. Ten minutes later he was Eastbound on the Kensington Expressway.

He arrived on Wilson Drive in Clarence and did a drive through. To call it a trailer park would be do it a disservice. They were older manufactured homes that all seemed to be modestly landscaped and well maintained. He drove past number 27 and noticed a maroon Nissan in the driveway. It looked like Angela might be at home. Tom turned around and parked on the other side of the street. He took a quick look around and got out. As he reached the apron of the driveway the side door of the house swung open and a young looking girl with dishwater blond hair came out lighting a cigarette. When she looked up and saw Tom she lost interest in the lighter and looked slightly panicked.

Tom stopped in his tracks. "Angela?"

"Who are you?" Angela asked.

"My name is Tom Donovan. I'm a private

investigator."

Angela took a step back. "What do you want?"

Tom sensed that the girl was scared and on the verge of running back in the house if he took another step closer.

"Your brother-in-law hired me to find your sister," Tom told and tried to sound reassuring. "I just wanted to ask you a couple of questions."

Angela looked at Tom incredulously, stepped up towards the side door and put her hand on the latch. "I already told Gary's other friends I don't know where she is."

That was odd, Tom thought. Shields had said that he had called Angela. He didn't mention he had someone else out looking for Donna. Just then Tom heard a motor and tires coming to a halt behind him. Angela looked over his shoulder and seemed to grow even more concerned. Tom turned to look behind him.

A young guy about 6' 3 and over two hundred pounds was coming around the front of an old ford pickup truck with a ladder rack. He was glaring at Tom. He had work clothes and a cap on over his dark hair. "Who the fuck are you?" he asked by way of an introduction.

"Bobby," Angela said.

Bobby walked right up to Tom and glanced over at Angela. "Go inside baby," he said.

There was something about Bobby's manner Tom

noticed. He was all chivalry and tough guy on the outside, but Tom detected a certain nervousness, like Bobby wasn't sure if he was making the smart play.

"I just came out for a smoke and he was in the driveway," Angela said.

"Go inside and check on Layla," Bobby told her.

Tom heard the door open and close behind him. He maintained eye contact with Bobby, but had adopted a passive stance with his hands at his side palms out.

"I don't suppose I could try to explain why I'm here?" Tom asked.

"I don't know you," Bobby started. "But going by the look on my wife's face I think I know why your here."

"It's true. I am looking for your sister-in-law. I didn't know somebody else was here and obviously whoever that was upset your wife."

Bobby said nothing so Tom continued, "I am going to reach into my pocket and take out my ID." He pulled out his wallet and opened it showing Bobby his photo ID and private investigators license. Bobby glanced at them so quickly Tom wasn't sure if he had even seen them at all.

"So you're a private investigator. Who are you working for?" Bobby asked.

"Your Brother-in-law, Gary Shields," Tom said.

Bobby frowned and his body seemed to tense. "My wife already told that goon who followed her home from the dental clinic that she hasn't heard from Donna in two weeks. You guys sweating her isn't going to change that fact."

Whoa, hang on a second," Tom said. He saw one of the Cryer's neighbors looking over from the next driveway.

"Everything okay Bob?" the neighbor asked.

"Yeah, Mr. Ward. This guy was just leaving." He looked back at Tom. "He has the wrong house."

Tom put his wallet back and lowered his voice. "You got me wrong kid. I know Gary is mixed up in some questionable stuff and with some unpleasant people. I don't want to see anything happen to Donna or your wife. Take my card and tell Angela that if she thinks her sister is in trouble and knows anything that could help me get her out of it to call me."

Bobby looked at the card in Tom's hand and then up at Tom. "Fuck you," he spat. "Get out of here before I call the cops."

Tom put his hands up and took a step back. As he started towards his car he heard the Cryer's side door open and close again. The neighbor was still outside pushing a broom, pretending he hadn't been listening. He glanced up and Tom caught his eye.

"Have a nice day," Tom said. The neighbor grunted and went back to his sweeping.

Tom pulled out onto Main Street and wondered what had been said to the Cryers to put them on edge. Furthermore who had said it? Were there threats made? His trip out from the city had been pretty fruitless and he was wondering what to do next. He realized he was only a short distance from Joe Walczak's home in Amherst. He replayed the conversation he had had that morning with Hugh and Bob Stanley and wondered why he hadn't heard from Joe before he hired a lawyer. Of course Tom hadn't reached out to his ex partner either, but things were happening fast. He turned right on Transit Road instead of left and headed for Joe's house.

Joe lived in a modest ranch house off of Sheridan Drive on a quiet tree lined street. Tom never had trouble remembering which house it was because it was the only one on the block with a wheelchair ramp leading up to the front door. The sight of the ramp always gave Tom a little jab in the gut.

Tom stood on the stoop and noticed he felt a little clammy. He rang the bell and a moment later Joe's wife Lisa opened the door.

"Tommy, how are you?" Lisa asked and she smiled.

Tom looked back at Lisa. "I'm alright Lisa. How are you?"

Tom noticed that Lisa Walczak was not the same pretty, petite woman he had met out for drinks with Joe six years ago; she looked different. Her blue eyes had a sort of permanent sadness about them now, accentuated by the crow's feet that Tom hadn't noticed before. The last couple of years had weighed heavily on her.

Lisa moved out and gave him a quick hug and then stepped back. As she did so she bumped into something. She turned around and picked up her son Tyler who was looking at Tom suspiciously.

"Wow," Tom said. "Somebody's getting big."

"Ugh. I know it he is going to be big like his daddy," she responded and looked from the child to Tom. "Tyler, do you remember daddy's friend Mr. Donovan?" Tyler buried his face into his mother's shoulder.

That's odd, Tom thought. When Tyler was born almost four years ago Joe and Lisa had always referred to him in front of the kid as 'Uncle Tom'. It also dawned on him that they were still standing on the front porch.

Might as well cut to the chase, Tom thought. "Is Joe in?" he asked.

Lisa grimaced slightly and appeared to be thinking of what to say.

"Lisa, is Joe alright? Are you alright?"

"Tom, I'm sorry," she said. Tom noticed her eyes were tearing up slightly. "This isn't a good time."

Tom immediately felt remorseful and wished he had called first. Lisa had been through a lot and now here he was again adding to her misery.

"Lisa, I should have called...I'm sorry..." Tom trailed off.

"Who is it Leese?" Joe's voice came from somewhere in the house.

"I just need a second," Tom said. His guilt was put on hold by his desire to find out just what the hell was going on.

Lisa gave Tom a look he couldn't decipher and then turned to yell down the hall. "It's Tom," she said.

It was quiet for a moment and then Joe finally said, "Send him in."

Lisa stepped back and pointed down the hall. "He's in the spare room, down on the right," she said and took her son and went into the kitchen.

Tom walked into the Joe's homemade office that had previously been a spare bedroom. Joe had mentioned to Tom that he was trying to start a security consulting business last year but said he was having trouble getting people to take a guy in a wheelchair seriously, ex-cop or not. Joe was seated behind his desk that faced the door.

"Tom Donovan. What brings you out of the big, bad city?" Joe asked.

Tom looked at his old partner. His eyes were bloodshot and it looked like he hadn't slept in a couple of days.

"I thought we should talk Joe," Tom said.

"About what? The old days? Fishing? Pussy?"

Tom frowned. It was unusual for Joe to be profane, especially with his wife possibly within earshot. He saw an empty glass on Joe's desk. "No, the lawsuit."

Joe put up his hands. "I can't," he said.

"What do you mean, you can't?"

Joe looked down at his desktop and seemed to try to compose himself. "Sorry Tom. My lawyer told me not to talk to anybody. Not even you."

"That's bullshit, Joe," Tom said, his voice rising.

"That's what I said, but he said we're better off with separate counsel," Joe told him.

"Did he say why? Wouldn't we be better off pooling our resources?"

Joe looked up at Tom ever so briefly and then back down. "Not according to him," he began. "Look Tom. He's coming out here tomorrow. I will ask him one more time, but as for now he made me promise him that I don't say a word to anybody, you, Lisa, my dad, anybody."

Just then Tyler squeezed past Tom and went around the desk and spoke to his father, "Mommy wants to know if your friend is going to have dinner with us."

Joe looked like he was getting misty eyed. He gazed up at Tom with a look that said he wished he were anywhere but where he was right now.

"Tell your mom thanks, Tyler," Tom said. "But I have to go." The little boy left the room.

Tom looked back at Joe. "Okay Joe, fine. But please, if something comes up and you need to talk for God's sake call me."

"Thanks Tommy, I will," Joe said quietly and forced a smile.

On his way out he stuck his head in the kitchen and waved to Lisa. She looked up at him sadly.

"Joe told me about the lawyer." he said. Lisa looked puzzled. Tom went on, "If you or Joe needs anything, anything at all, call me."

Lisa came over and gave Tom another hug.

Tom said, "I am so sorry Lisa. I've been a pretty lousy partner."

They stepped apart and now it was Tom's turn to get misty eyed.

"Take care of yourself Tom," she said and smiled up at him. "We'll be okay."

Tom walked out to his car feeling just about as guilty as he felt on that cold March night two years before.

Chapter 11

Tom stopped at a donut shop on Sheridan and went into the men's room to wash his face. He knew he should probably eat something, but his stomach was still in knots. He ordered a large coffee to go and went out to his car.

He called the agency to check in, but Cal was out of the office. Tom told Grace to tell Cal that he had spoken to the sister, but nothing useful had come from it. He didn't mention being confronted by the husband or the fact that the Cryers seemed to be scared of something or somebody.

Tom sat in his car and tried to collect his thoughts. He thought about calling Grace back to see if she would have Cal call him so he could ask him some more questions about Shield's partner Manzella, but he decided to wait on that.

Tom's phone buzzed and he picked it up. The caller ID said 'restricted', but Tom answered it anyway.

"Yeah."

"Tom, it's Brian Dinkle."

"What's up?"

"I think I have a line on Donna Shields' guardian angel."

"You know who she is?" Tom asked.

"I'm pretty sure I have the right girl," Brian responded.

Tom pulled out his notebook. "Okay, what do you have?"

"Well after I enhanced the still," Brian began. "I had from the surveillance video, which took some time I must say, I got a pretty good image of her. I did some digging through Donna Shields' past, which was pretty damned boring, and I was just about to give up when I found a picture in the University of Rochester's student paper that looks a lot like your mystery woman."

"Is it a picture of her and Donna together?" Tom asked.

"No such luck. I did put the pictures side by side and I'll be damned if it's not the same person. The picture from the school paper was of the Navy ROTC candidates from 1997. That would have put her at the University the same time as Donna."

"Hmm, do you have a name?"

"Yeah, Katrina Bedford of Rochester NY," Brian answered.

"Is she still in Rochester?"

"Nope. Found an item in the Rochester *Democrat and Chronicle* that said she was going into the Navy right after graduation. She was in six years and then got out on a medical discharge."

"Medical," Tom muttered. "What was that?"

"Her DOD file didn't go into a lot of detail," Brian aid.

Tom winced and reminded himself the less he knew about how Brian came up with information the better.

Brian continued, "Here's a fun fact. She was accepted into the SEAL training school."

"Shit," Tom said. "GI Jane."

"Something like that. Didn't say if she finished or not"

Tom thought for a second. "What was the date of the discharge?"

"May 15, 2006," Brian said.

"So where has she been for the last six years?"

"No idea," Brian said. "No address, no credit score, no arrest records."

"Any family still in Rochester?" Tom asked.

Brian clicked a couple of buttons on his keyboard. "Not in Rochester. Her mother was never married and she moved to Florida in 2001."

"That's it?"

"Well I am glad you asked," Brian said. "I found some court records that stated that Katrina's mother had lost custody of her and she went into foster care. She was with a couple of different families, but it looks like she settled in with a Mr. and Mrs. Penrod in Batavia."

"How did you..." Tom stopped himself. "And?"

"Mr. Penrod passed away last year, but Mrs. Anne Penrod still lives in Batavia."

Tom checked his watch, it was 5:45. He could be in Batavia by 6:30.

"You are amazing, Mr. Dinkle," Tom told him. "Let me have the address."

At 6:45 Tom drove by the address on South Swan Street in Batavia that Brian had given him. He did a moderately slow drive by of the small Cape Cod style home and saw that there were no cars in the driveway and the garage door was closed. Had he driven all this way for nothing? This was the only lead he had right now so he decided to come back after dark and watch the house for a while. He found a pizza place on Ellicot Street that sold pizza by the slice and got the local paper. He killed a little more time with another cup of coffee and then decided it was dark enough to go back to South Swan and check on the house.

Tom pulled his car into a Church parking lot that was about fifty yards from the Penrod house. He parked next to a couple of cars on the edge of the lot that looked like they were just using the lot so they didn't have to park on the street and risk getting sideswiped. From his vantage point Tom could see the front door and a light on in the window next to it. He sat for a while and wondered how he would explain his presence to a curious passerby or worse, police officer. His phone buzzed, restricted ID again.

"What's up, Brian?" Tom answered.

"Hello?" It was a woman's voice.

"This is Donovan."

"Oh, I didn't know if I should call your office or this number."

Tom was trying to place the voice. "I'm here. Who is this?"

"Oh, sorry. It's Candy. From the club."

Tom had almost forgotten he had given her his card. "Oh hey, what's up?"

Tom heard a small child in the background. Jesus Christ, he thought, she has a kid and she is practically a kid herself.

"I don't want to get in trouble," Candy said.

"What is it?"

The phone was silent for a while then Tom heard Candy take a breath. "I think Mrs. Shields is in trouble," she said.

"What do you mean?" Tom asked.

"Well, I really don't know her that well," Candy said, almost a whisper. "She only comes to the club once in a while. But I like her. She is the only one who doesn't treat the girls like shit and she never puts on airs. You know, like she was better that all of us."

She was getting off topic. Tom tried to bring her back. "Candy, what makes you think she's in trouble?"

"Well I was on stage the night before last when she

came in. She didn't say a word to anyone, which is unusual. Usually she will smile or say hi, but not that night. She just came in with this worried look on her face and went upstairs. I was just finishing up when she came back down and made a bee line for the door."

"Did she have anything with her?" Tom asked.

Candy thought for a moment. Again, Tom heard the babble of a toddler in the background. "I think she had a bag or an envelope, now that you mention it."

"And did she talk to anybody?"

"No," Candy said quickly. "But Mike followed her out. That's why I think she's in trouble. He scares me."

Manzella, Tom thought. "Listen Candy, first of all; is that your real name?"

"No, it's Rachel," she said.

"Listen Rachel," Tom said. "I don't want to scare you, but I think you are working for some pretty bad people. I want you to promise me that you won't tell anybody about calling me."

Tom heard her sniffle and say, "I know they're bad, really bad."

Tom hesitantly asked, "What do you mean?"

"They have a place," she began with a slight quiver in her voice.

"What place, Rachel?"

"It's out in the country. They call it 'The Farm'"

"What do they do there?"

Rachel was trying to contain herself, "They have parties...we go out there...with the VIPs."

Tom was getting the picture. "Who goes out there Rachel? Mr. Shields? Mike?"

She sniffled again. "Mostly Mike, but yeah Gary goes out there too, but he never gets with the girls."

What a gentleman, Tom thought. "Okay, Rachel take it easy." He gave her a second. "Do you know where this place is?"

"Well, I've only been down there in the limo so I never paid that much attention." She thought for a second. "I do know we take a right off of Route 5 and I saw a water tower with the letter F on it once."

"Just an F?"

"There were other letters but I could only see the F from the car."

Tom took a breath. His mind was trying to figure out if there was any connection between Shields' and Manzella's rural whorehouse and Donna Shields.

"Rachel how does it work? When the high rollers go out to the Farm."

"You know Larry? The guy you beat up last night? His brother Donny takes us out and opens the place up and then we have to stay out there all night." Her voice trembled again. "Then there's the drugs at the club and the farm house."

"What drugs?"

"Mike sells drugs out of the club, coke, meth, and he uses them to get the girls to turn tricks. A lot of the girls who work there spend most of their tip money on drugs. He's been working on me, but I told him they make me sick." Tom remembered her dilated pupils and cringed.

"Have you ever noticed a burglar alarm or anything by the door at the farm house?"

"I'm not sure, there might be. But there is a really creepy guy who lives on the property and he has a couple of mean looking dogs."

Tom's mind was kicking into overdrive. "Rachel do you have to go to work tonight?"

"No I had to call in. My little girl has a fever and my mom had to work."

"Alright, good. I think you should steer clear of that place for a while."

"I gotta go in tomorrow or they're gonna fire me."

"Rachel."

"I need the money while I can get it. My mom's lease is up next month and we need to come up with eight hundred bucks for a deposit on a new place."

Tom felt his stomach tighten again. What the hell had he gotten this poor girl into?

"Okay, listen. Throw my card out and forget you ever called me for now."

"But…"

"Rachel, I have a feeling that things are going to

happen in the next couple of days, and the best thing for you to do is to not be noticed. I want you to lay low and I'll contact you when it's okay."

Silence for a moment and then Rachel said weakly, "Okay Tom, thank you." She hung up.

Thank me for what? Tom wondered.

A man walking a dog walked right by Tom's car just then but didn't seem to notice him. Tom remembered where he was and looked down the street towards the foste mother's house. The light in the front window was out. Shit, he thought. Did somebody come home while I was distracted? Am I losing my touch? His legs were starting to cramp so he decided now was as good a time as any so he climbed out of the car. He decided to leave his phone in the car so it wouldn't vibrate or light up at an inopportune moment.

He made his way at a medium pace down the street. The dog walker had disappeared into a house a few doors down from the Penrod residence. When he arrived in front of the Cape he took a quick look around and seeing no one else out on the street, headed up the driveway. He wanted to check the garage first. It sat back on the property slightly away from the house. He stayed close to the house and stayed below the windows in case someone was looking outside. There was a row of windows across one panel of the garage door. Tom cupped his hands over the side of his eyes and peered inside. In the faint light that made it up the driveway from the streetlight Tom thought he saw the roof of a white sedan. It could be the same car he had seen at Showgirls, but he couldn't see enough of it to be sure. He looked back at the house's windows he had just passed; they were dark and showed no signs of movement. He went to the corner of the garage and looked in the back yard. There was light coming from one of the rear windows.

Tom crept along the back wall towards the light being careful not to trip or kick anything. It was a cool night but he could feel a trickle of sweat running down his back. He reached the window of the room with the light on. Tom came out of his crouch slowly, letting his eyes adjust to the light coming from inside. It was a bedroom. He thought he heard a voice but didn't see anybody.

He heard a sound to his left. He spun in time to see a small dark shadow coming towards him with its right hand reaching up towards him. Tom brought his left hand up as quickly as he could surprising her and knocking the taser out of her hand. As he did so his left foot slipped slightly and he tried to catch himself. A flash of metal from her left hand and the collapsible baton struck Tom in the side of his head. Stunned, he fell face first onto the cold, wet grass. Before he had a chance to move she was on top of him, knee in his back, his arm bent behind him while she held by his thumb at a very awkward angle.

"Trina?" Tom heard a voice from what he thought was the side of the house."

Katrina hissed in Tom's ear, "Move and I will break your thumb." And then slightly louder, "Back here. Bring the flashlight."

"Katrina," Tom said with what seemed like a mouthful of grass.

Tom felt intense pain as she bent his thumb up towards his neck. "Shut up," she said

"Okay, okay," Tom said wincing.

The flashlight the hit his eye and then Katrina asked Donna, "Who is he?"

Donna looked for a second and said, "I've never seen him before."

Trina lowered her head slightly towards Tom's ear again.

"Who are you?"

Tom closed his eyes and felt his head throb. "Donovan, I'm a PI."

Again the thumb was bent. Tom was sure one more time and it would break.

"Okay, listen Donovan. You tell Gary that we have something of his that he and his friend Mike are going to want back very badly. All we want is the package that he has regarding Donna. We make a clean swap and everybody walks away happy."

"I don't…" Tom started to say.

This time she drove her knee into his kidney. At least it's not the thumb he thought.

"Shhh," Katrina hissed. "It doesn't matter what you think, you are off the case. Do you know what this is?" Tom felt something being pressed into the back of his skull.

"Probably a gun?"

"Right. Just deliver the message and If I ever see you again I am going to kill you. Oh, and if the lady who lives in this house ever sees you or any of Gary's other asshole friends I am going to kill you." She got off of him while still pressing the gun to his head and took his wallet out of his back pocket, "Mr. Thomas H. Donovan of St James Place."

"Can I get up now?" Tom asked

Just a second sweetie," Katrina said. Tom hadn't seen it but Donna Shields had retrieved the taser for Katrina. "Give us a couple of minutes."

Tom felt the electrodes hit his neck and the shock go through him. It felt like a flame shot through his entire body and he had the sensation that his body actually left the ground. After the red receded to black he lost consciousness.

Chapter 12

Tom was back in uniform and in a sitting in a squad car idling on East Ferry. He suddenly had the sensation that somebody was watching him and looked around outside of the squad car. Nobody there. A call came over the radio and he didn't catch it. There was a knock on the driver's side window that startled Tom and he looked up to see his father. Big Tom just looked into the car and didn't say anything. Then Tom heard a purring noise.

He opened his eyes and saw a stray cat about six inches away from his face. He moved his arm and the cat bolted into the darkness. He was still lying face down in Anne Penrod's back yard. He had no idea how long he had been out for, but at least it was still dark out.

Tom felt the burn on his neck and ran his hand across the knot on the side of his head. He felt the dampness of the ground soaking through his clothes and wondered if he hadn't pissed himself. He had to get out of there. He pushed himself up on his hands and his knees felt his stomach lurch and he threw up immediately. After taking a moment to compose himself he felt the back of his pants and remembered Katrina had taken his wallet. He checked the ground around him and didn't see it so he got up and walked shakily down the driveway and out in to the street. He was relieved to find he still had his keys. He slumped into his car and checked his phone, it was 3:21 AM He took an unused fast food napkin from the glove box and gently pressed it against the bump on his head and it came away clean. He started the car and headed towards the Thruway.

He reached his apartment and, after taking a long hot shower and improvising an ice pack for his throbbing head Tom grabbed a beer and headed off to the recliner with his notebook. He wrote down all of the things he could remember from his conversation with Candy/Rachel regarding the 'farm'. Then on the next page he wrote the name Donna and underlined it. Under that he wrote: "What does she want from Shields?" He wrote the name Katrina Bedford under that and circled it. He sat back and closed his eyes for a moment but then the exhaustion took over and he fell fast asleep.

Tom's phone buzzed on the table next to his chair. He looked at the clock on the mantle. It was 10:10 in the morning. The sun was shining in the living room window and the light hurt his eyes. He fumbled for the phone.

"I sure hate to disturb you Thomas." It was Cal.

Tom cleared the sleep out of his throat. "Hey boss."

"I'm still waiting on some kind of progress report," Cal said. "Or are you taking today off?"

Tom shook his head and tried to clear it. "I saw

Donna Shields last night."

"What? Where?" Cal stammered.

"She was holed up in Batavia with her friend from the surveillance video," Tom said.

"You said 'was'. She's not there now?"

Tom didn't think he wanted to go into detail on how he had gotten his ass kicked by a 5'5" woman who he probably outweighed by fifty pounds. "I was doing a little surveillance on her friend's foster mother's house and the surveillance was compromised."

Cal's voice became agitated. "And why would you be doing any kind of surveillance on anybody without telling me?"

"Take it easy Cal," Tom said. "Brian had come up with an ID on Donna's friend from the surveillance video and gave me a lead on a local connection. I didn't think it was anything so I took a ride out there just to eliminate it, but they were there." Tom stopped to see how that would go over.

"And what do you mean by 'compromised'?"

Tom hesitated, again not sure about how much to tell Cal. He was in deep and wanted to try and sort things out with a minimum of interference. "I think they spotted me. I can't be sure but there wasn't really a good place to set up and watch the house. I think they made me."

"Then what?" Cal said and his voice had lowered a bit.

"They took off in a white sedan," Tom told him. "I followed for a little while, but I lost them at a light. I think they were headed for the Thruway, but when I got on they were nowhere in sight."

Cal seemed to think for a moment. "Alright, what's next? Mr. Shields is calling every couple of hours and I want to tell him something positive."

"Tell him we identified her companion and are looking for her to tip us off where Donna might be."

"Is that the truth?" Cal asked. "Do you have any other leads?"

Tom thought for a moment, unsure and then he said, "Yes."

Tom heard Cal's other line buzz. He put Tom hold and then came back and said, "I have to take another call. Get your ass in here and give me everything you have."

"Right boss." Tom heard the line go dead.

Another shower. Tom still had a noticeable lump on his head that showed through his close-cropped hair. The taser burn looked much better except for two small red marks on the side of his neck. He put a ball cap on and headed out. Driving down Delaware and thinking about everything that had happened the day before he remembered that he had not called Bob Stanley about drafting the response to the lawsuit. He pulled Stanley's card out of his jacket pocket pulled over and punched in the number. The receptionist put him on hold for a few minutes and then put him through.

"Tom?" Stanley said.

"Hi, Bob. Sorry, I didn't get back to you last night."

"That's okay, I am just glad you called," Stanley replied.

"Listen Bob," Tom began. "I think I am going to need your help after all, at least with the reply."

Stanley was quiet for a moment and then said, "I'm glad to hear that. Are you busy right now? My morning appearance was postponed and I think we should talk."

"Actually, I have to go into a meeting with Cal."

"This is pretty important, Tom. I think we should do this sooner rather than later."

Tom noticed Stanley's tone was even more serious than usual. "Alright. I can be there in fifteen," Tom said.

"Great. Tell Noreen to send you right in."

Stanley, Morris and Krebs had an office in the Ellicot Square building a short walk from the courthouse. Tom parked in the garage nearby and went in.

"You must be Mr. Donovan," a plump middle-aged woman said when Tom entered.

"Yes."

She stood up and led Tom down a hall and into Stanley's office. Stanley sat behind his large oak desk typing something into his computer. He had his jacket off revealing an immaculately pressed white shirt. He looked up and took off his reading glasses.

"Tom. Have a seat. Coffee? Water?" Stanley

sounded cordial.

"No, thanks," Tom replied.

Stanley looked over Tom's shoulder and said, "Thank you Noreen." Tom heard the door close behind him.

Stanley sat back, picked up a Cross pen and studied it. "I think we have a problem," he said. He returned the pen to the desk and looked at Tom.

"What kind of problem?"

"While I usually don't give rumors much credence," Stanley said. "This one came from a reliable source."

Tom gestured for Stanley to continue.

"It looks like Joe Walczak is changing his story about the circumstances surrounding you and Derrick Trent."

"What are you talking about?" Tom asked.

"He is prepared to give a statement to the plaintiff's counsel that you were out to get Trent and the shooting may have been premeditated."

Tom was stunned. Why would Joe say something like that? Was the rumor even true? "Bullshit," he finally said.

Stanley sighed and then went on. "Look Tom, I am stepping way out of bounds by first of all having this information, and then compounding it by sharing it with you. I don't want to get in to how I know this, but my source has never led me astray before."

Tom was speechless. Stanley reached over to the

corner of his desk and picked up a piece of paper. "I took the liberty of drafting your response to the suit," he began. "It's just basically a denial of all of the allegations, pretty standard. I can file it for you today and buy you some time while we work this out."

Tom took the letter and tried to read it, but he couldn't focus. What the hell was happening? Two days ago none of this would have been comprehensible, but after seeing Joe and his erratic behavior yesterday maybe some of it was true. He handed the letter back to Stanley.

"File it," Tom said.

Stanley shook his head in the affirmative. "Good. I'm going over to the courthouse after lunch. In the meantime I'm having my paralegal pull the transcripts from the original grand jury."

Tom stood up still dazed but now feeling angry. "Thanks, Bob. I have to get going."

Bob Stanley stood himself and nodded. "Okay, Tom. I know this comes as a blow, but we can get you through this."

Tom walked around Downtown for about a half hour trying to calm himself down. He thought about calling Joe but decided not to. Some day after all this was over he would sit down with his ex partner and get this all straightened out. Right now the best thing to do was let Stanley handle it. He went back to the garage and got his car.

Twenty minutes later he was back at Frederickson and Associates. He heard raised voices coming from Cal's office as he passed by Grace's desk.

"What's going on in there?" he said gesturing over Grace's shoulder.

"Cal and Travis are coming to an understanding," she said looking back at her computer screen.

Travis Parker was another one of the agencies investigators. He was also Cal's nephew and a former gang member. After seeing his best friend die in front of him when he was nineteen his uncle had helped him see the error of his ways. Cal first helped him go to college and then offered him a job. While on the surface it looked like pure nepotism Tom had learned that Travis was smart and resourceful and had a decent head on his shoulders. And as far as preferential treatment was concerned, Cal seemed to be the hardest on his nephew. It was an interesting dynamic because Travis could take anything the old man dished out. Travis had dreams of going to law school, but right now he was trying to pay off some debts.

Tom could still hear Cal, railing on about something. "Your husband has a very thorough way of making sure things are understood."

Grace glanced up and gave a slight smile.

Tom went into his office and got out his notebook. He skimmed through the pages until he got to the page he had on Donna and Katrina. Katrina had mentioned that they had something that Gary Shields and Mike Manzella would want back. That had to be what Donna had taken from the club on Monday. And they were willing to trade it for something that was of particular concern to Donna. Right now it didn't matter what that was. All Tom knew was that Donna Shields was scared enough to bring her violent little friend with her for protection when she went to the club to look for it. Tom thought about calling Gary Shields and telling him about the offer Katrina had whispered into his ear last night. The thought disagreed with him. The more he found out about the world that Shields operated in the more he disliked him. He needed more time and a few more answers.

He looked at the preceding page in the notebook. He had scribbled a few things about the 'farm' that Candy had told him about. His curiosity got the better of him and he took his notebook into Brian's office. Brian was pulling his coat on.

"What's up, Tom?" Brian asked.

"Are you headed out?"

"Yeah, did you need something?"

Tom gestured towards the large hi-definition monitor on Brian's desk. "I want to check something out on Google-earth and I thought I might get a better image on your screen than my little fifteen inch monitor."

Brian frowned and said, "I just logged off."

Tom was puzzled for a moment and then understood.

"Look Brian I swear," Tom said. "I just want to check the maps. As soon as I am done I'll log off and lock your office."

"I don't..."

Tom went on, "I could give a rat's ass what you do in here. Your domain is like Vegas. What happens in Brian's hovel stays in Brian's hovel."

Brian thought for a moment. "Okay. Jeez, you make me sound like some kind of perverted freak. Wait out here a second." Brian went back to his desk while Tom waited at the doorway.

Just calling them like I see them, Tom thought.

Brian picked up his backpack and started to leave. "It's all yours chief," he said.

"Thanks Brian. I promise to keep your disturbing secrets safe," Tom replied.

"You are hilarious," Brian said dryly as he left the room.

Tom sat down at Brian's desk. Was he imagining it or did he smell weed? He looked at his notebook at the page he had made from Candy's phone call. He knew she had said that the place was in the country off of Route 5. She hadn't mentioned the Thruway or going through Downtown (of course, he realized, he hadn't asked her) so he decided to look to the South first.

'Water tower -F-,' his notes said. He opened up the map web site and zeroed in on Southern Erie County.

Fredonia? Candy had referred to it as "Out in the country," so Fredonia was probably too densely populated. That left Forrestville and Farnham. Tom suddenly had a vague recollection of going past a water tower as a boy when his parents took him and his sister to the beach, which would make it Farnham. He converted from the map image to the satellite and in a few minutes found the tower on the corner of Route 5 and Lotus Point Road. He pulled back on the image a little and tried to find a property that would fit Candy's description of having a main structure and a smaller building where the caretaker lived.

The first one he saw didn't look too promising. The larger structure appeared to be a barn that was in pretty bad shape. The second one though made more sense. It was a half-mile West on Lotus Point Road and it appeared as though the property was fairly well maintained. It looked as though the surrounding grounds may have been an orchard at one time. Maybe it still was, that would be an excellent cover for a brothel. Tom zoomed in and decided that it was probably his best bet.

He checked his watch. It was 4:30. He considered the thought of going out to Farnham and having a look around. What about the caretaker and his dogs? He would need an excuse to be nosing around. He made a printout of a map of the area, logged off Brian's computer and went back to his office.

How could he get past the caretaker and have a look

at the farm? He sat down at his desk and looked up hoping for inspiration. There was nothing up there but acoustic ceiling tile. His gaze came down and landed on Sherry Palkowski's desk. No way, he thought. Would she? Tom got up and went over to Sherry's desk, opened a drawer and found one of her business cards.

He walked briskly down the hall and into the reception area. Grace looked up and caught him at the door and said, "Tom, Cal wants to talk to you but he's on the phone right now. Can you wait?"

"Ooh, I just got a lead on the car Donna Shields was driving the other night," Tom told her. "Tell him not to worry. I'm not going to do anything stupid and I'll call him after I check it out."

Grace frowned and said, "Okay, I'll tell him the part about the car and you calling him. But I'm not going to tell him the part about not worrying or you doing something stupid."

"Your words hurt me Grace," Tom said as he went out the door.

Chapter 13

Tom put on a pair of slacks, button down shirt and his best blazer. He looked at himself in the mirror and thought maybe I can pull this off. He thought about the last couple of nights, he had been in a fistfight with a large, angry bouncer and zapped unconscious by a former Navy SEAL candidate.

Tom had briefly thought about renting a car, sort of upgrading his ride, but he realized he didn't have the time. He would have to try do this with the way things were.

Sherry had called him back shortly after he had left her a message saying was just leaving the gym. At first she was skeptical until Tom appealed to her sense of citizenship and her feminist leanings. After he explained what went on at the Farm and told her about how scared Donna and Candy seemed to be she reluctantly agreed to help.

Tom pulled up in front of Sherry's Allentown apartment at 7:15. He was about to get out and ring the bell when she came out the front door. He restarted the car and Sherry climbed in. Tom looked over and noticed Sherry's coat had opened. She was wearing a blue silk blouse and short black skirt that showed off quite a bit of leg. She also had on a pair of high-heeled black shoes. Tom pulled his gaze up and looked at her face. She was wearing a generous amount of makeup, which Tom had never seen her do before. Actually he couldn't recall her wearing makeup at all. Her blond hair was down around her shoulders and she had teased it out a little. She was wearing perfume too. Tom wasn't an expert but it smelled nice and expensive. It reminded him of a scent Erica, his ex-girlfriend, used to wear.

Sherry picked up on his look. "So, do I look like a stripper?" she asked.

Tom didn't know what to say. He had learned that with women sometimes there were no right answers. He started the car and pulled away from the curb.

"It's just that you look...different," he stammered.

Sherry smiled and said, "Yeah, it's not the kind of image I go for at work."

"I guess not."

"Actually the shoes and the blouse are mine. I borrowed the skirt from my roommate. It's a little shorter than I like but I was going for a certain look."

Tom did everything in his power not to look over at Sherry's legs. He knew she worked out all the time but he had never seen the results. "Well, it's a different look for you," he told her.

"What, don't you think lesbians like to get dressed

up?" she asked and smiled at him.

The look of surprise on Tom's face must have been noticeable because Sherry picked up on it right away. She gave a little laugh and said, "Some detective you are."

Tom frowned and said, "Well, I never really thought about it. We really never got into each other's personal lives." It was true. Tom and Sherry had shared an office since Tom started at the agency. The conversations they had had consisted mostly of small talk. Tom contributed part of this to the fact that on his worst days he considered himself damaged goods and he sensed that Sherry wanted to keep her distance.

"Still, with all of your powers of deduction..." she teased.

Now Tom smiled. "One thing I have learned is to not make assumptions about anybody. You have to go with the facts in front of you or you may get into trouble."

Sherry seemed to consider this. "And what facts do you have about me?" she asked.

"From what I have seen and what Cal tells me I think you would make a good cop," Tom told her.

Sherry looked out straight ahead through the windshield. "Thanks."

"No, really. I think you have the perfect temperament and work ethic. The thing is you don't know for sure until you get out on the job. I went through the academy with some guys I thought were going to fly up the ladder and more than a few of them crashed and burned in one way or another."

They were on the Sky Way heading south. After a while Sherry looked over at Tom and said, "Do you miss it?"

Tom thought about that. No one had asked him that in a while. "I do. Probably just as much as the day I got fired."

Sherry seemed to be thinking of something.

"Go ahead," Tom said. "If there is something you want to ask I think now's a good time. It seems like we know surprisingly little about each other for sharing an office for nine months."

Sherry didn't smile. Finally she said, "I don't want this to come out the wrong way."

"You want to know about Trent?"

Another pause. "Actually no," Sherry began. "I have no idea what I would've done or what was going through your mind that night, and I think it's bullshit if anybody thinks that they do."

Tom looked back at her. "But?"

"No, if I had to say anything about that I would say that you got screwed. And what they did to that little girl."

"What is it then?" Tom asked.

"Did your uncle get you on the force?" she asked him.

So, that's what was on her mind, Tom thought. "He always denied it, but I don't think that's completely true. I was in the top three of my class at the academy, but it didn't hurt that Sam Dipietro was a captain and my uncle. I could understand how someone in your position might resent that."

Sherry thought about that for a second and then said, "I know you wouldn't have been the first one to get in as a legacy. Was it hard?"

Tom hadn't expected that as a follow up question. "Well, it was a little at first. Everybody thinks you got in without earning it, so they are just waiting for you to screw up. Then they can say, 'I told you so.' You're under a little more scrutiny than the other rookies so you have to work that much harder to prove yourself."

"You spent most of your time in E district didn't you?" she asked.

"Eight out of the ten years I was on the job."

"Not exactly the most plum assignment."

Tom let out a short laugh. "The first thing you used to see when you went in the back door was a sign that said 'Welcome to Hell.' It wasn't quite that bad, but it was busy. Not to sound like a cliché but it was the area that I thought I could make the biggest difference. A lot of people have written the East Side off but they forget that despite all the poverty and crime that there are still human beings down there trying to live their lives."

"That only sounds slightly clichéd," Sherry said and laughed a little.

"Well what about you? Why law enforcement?"

Sherry put her head back and thought. "Good question. I think the short answer would be to paraphrase what you said, I want to make a difference."

"Did you always want to be a cop?" Tom asked.

Sherry laughed again and said, "No when I was younger I thought I wanted to be a teacher, but after doing some babysitting when I was in high school I had the revelation that I really don't like kids all that much."

Tom smiled and told her, "That's good. A lot of the teachers I had at St. Ignatius School didn't like kids either."

Just before eight they were doing a slow cruise down Lotus Point Road. Sherry checked Tom's aerial printout and said, "I think we just passed it."

"What? I didn't see anything."

"There was a driveway about fifty yards back on the left."

Tom turned the car around and sure enough there was a narrow gravel driveway cut between a row of trees that lined the road. He turned in and after a short distance they entered a clearing. Right in front of them was a small house with new siding that looked like it may have been some type of carriage house in a previous life. Fifty yards behind it and to the left was a large old farmhouse that also looked like it had been recently refurbished.

"Ready?" he asked as he turned off his phone.

"Did you mention something about dogs?"

"Yeah, Rachel the dancer said this guy keeps a couple of big ones out here."

Sherry reached into her purse and came out with a can of pepper spray. "I don't like kids or dogs," she said. "Let's go."

As they walked to the house the dogs started barking from inside. Tom noticed Sherry tense slightly. He had to sympathize with her though. He had been bitten badly once on patrol when he and his partner stumbled onto a dog-fighting ring.

"Now remember this whole plan is counting on this guy being really gullible," Tom said.

"That's reassuring," Sherry responded. "Where are you going?"

Tom had ducked over to the side of the house. He removed a pair of wire cutters from his jacket pocket and snipped the wires underneath the phone box. "We don't want any interruptions. Oh, open up your coat."

The inside door had opened before they had a chance to knock. A overweight man who to be about sixty years old wearing a dirty T-shirt looked out at them and said something that they couldn't hear because the dog that was next to him was barking and trying to get through the screen door. The man kicked the dog in the side silencing him and stepped outside. "Can I help you?" He was missing a couple of teeth.

Tom took the lead. "Yeah, my man, Mike has been trying to call you for an hour." Tom knew this was the big gamble.

"For what? Waddya mean trying to call? I been in all day."

"Party tonight," Tom said, smiling at Sherry. "He said you would open up the house but your phone is out of service or something."

The caretaker scratched his stubble covered chin and said, "Where's Donny?"

"Mike sent him up to the Falls to pick up some people at the casino."

The caretaker looked at Tom and then past him to Sherry. His eyes locked on her for a moment and then he looked back at Tom. "Hang on a minute," he said. He turned towards the house.

Tom looked at Sherry and shrugged. He noticed she still had the pepper spray in her hand. Tom pointed at it and whispered, "Put that away." Sherry frowned and put it back in her purse.

"What if he has a cell phone?" she hissed.

Tom shrugged again. "He doesn't look like the type."

"Weren't you just saying something about not making assumptions?"

Before he could reply he heard the screen door open and the dogs started barking again. Tom turned around to see the man give the lead dog another kick. "I said shut up," he yelled as the dog shrunk back.

He turned and looked at Tom. "God damned phone is dead."

"I guess that's why Mike couldn't get a hold of you."

"Well, you're gonna have to wait."

Tom said, "Goddamn it. Here, I'll call him. He pulled out his cell phone and looked at the blank screen. "Goddamned battery." He turned and looked at Sherry. "Sweetheart, let me use your phone."

Sherry looked back at Tom and gave a little shiver. "Sorry, I left it in the dressing room at the club."

Tom said, "Shit," and looked back at the caretaker. Time to really start acting. "C'mon pal. Mike said this was all set up. Donny isn't going to be here for another hour and it's freezing out here."

The caretaker didn't budge. He just looked impassively at Tom.

Tom jerked his thumb back towards Sherry and said, "Are you going to make a sweet girl like Crystal wait in the car?"

The caretaker looked past Tom at Sherry. Tom couldn't see what she was doing but whatever it was working. The man's beady eyes locked on to her and seemed to be stuck there. Time for the Hail Mary, Tom thought and he pulled a money clip out of his pocket and peeled off a fifty-dollar bill.

The caretaker looked down briefly at the money as though Tom had woke him up from a trance.

"For your trouble," Tom said.

The caretaker looked at the bill for a while and then back at Sherry. "I never seen you before young lady," He said to her. "Are you new?"

Sherry stepped up next to Tom. She was turning up the charm without overdoing it. "I started last month. This is my first time here though." She smiled, stepped a little closer to the man raised her chin and said, "Why, don't I look like the type?"

The old man's blotchy skin turned red. "No., I mean, actually you look a lot classier than them other girls."

Sherry put her right hand on the man's cheek. "That is the nicest thing anybody's said to me since I started working there."

The man's face was almost crimson now. He looked at the ground and then at Tom. He then reached out and took the fifty. "Alright," he said. "Pull your car back by the house and I'll get the keys."

The sun had almost completely disappeared over the tree line. The caretaker let them in and disarmed the alarm from the panel by the front door. He then unlocked the bar in the living room and then said he was going back to the house to wait for Donny. He left with one last leer at Sherry.

"That was an Oscar worthy performance 'Crystal'," Tom said as he scanned the room. The room had a bucolic farmhouse feel with a few updates. Over the stone fireplace was a large flat screen TV. The furniture was all new and comfortable looking but still looked country. The hardwood floor was either new or had been stripped and refinished by a pro.

Sherry was on the other side of the room. "Thanks. You too, big pimp," she said. "I want to see how you report that fifty dollars on your expense sheet."

Tom shook his head. "I'm just glad he didn't hold out for more. That fifty was wrapped around a bunch of ones and fives. Actually it was mostly ones."

"So, what are we looking for and where do we start?"

Tom reminded himself that they had better move quickly. He had no idea how much time they had. "I'm looking for an office with desk or a safe or filing cabinet," he said. "Do me a favor, you start down here. I'm going to look upstairs."

"Right," Sherry responded.

Tom climbed the staircase and looked down the hall. There were three doors on either side of the passage. He opened the first door on his right and found himself in a marble tiled bathroom complete with a large whirlpool tub and walk-in shower with an adjustable shower massage head. He turned to the door on his right. The door was locked so he decided to move on at least for the moment. Three of the remaining four rooms almost looked like honeymoon suites at a bed and breakfast, complete with ice buckets and champagne flutes. The last room on the right was quite the eye opener. The room was dark until Tom pushed the dimmer switch up.

It was not so much as a bed as a worktable with a metal headboard, Tom thought. The metal looked to be pretty marked up from handcuffs or some other kind of restraints. On the wall there was a rack with what appeared to be an assortment of riding crops, leather straps, varied gags and a few things Tom didn't recognize. There was an armoire across from the foot of the bed that didn't want to open when Tom tried it. He thought about forcing it for a moment to see if it held what he was looking for but decided that this didn't seem like the type of place that records would be kept.

He moved back down the hall to the locked door.

Sherry had just come up stairs and was shaking her head. "Quite the boy's club they have here," she muttered. "Pool table, brand new kitchen and a lounge with some of the nastiest porno mags I have ever seen."

Tom tried the door. It was definitely locked. He really didn't want to break into anything he didn't have too. He figured he and Sherry were already potentially in enough trouble.

"Here let me try something," Sherry said reaching in to her bag. She rummaged around the bottom of it for a moment and then pulled out a bobby pin. She stepped in front of Tom and stuck it in the lock.

Tom was doubtful but didn't want to say it out loud. "Well, the upstairs is about as quaint and lovely as can be except for the last room on the right," he said.

To Tom's surprise the door popped open. Sherry pushed it all the way and turned on the light. "My sister and I used to sneak into my parent's room and peak at our presents at Christmas time. They had the same crappy locks on their doors," she said.

Tom looked into the room. It was smaller than the other ones on the second floor due to the fact that a quarter of it was taken up by the stairwell. It was sparsely furnished with an older wooden desk, a few chairs and a worn looking couch. He didn't see a safe or file cabinet. He thought of something and turned to Sherry.

"The room down at the end on the right, there's a cabinet in it," Tom told her. "Can you use your breaking and entering skills to try to get a look inside? I'm going to take a quick look at the desk."

"Sure."

"Oh and Sherry, I should warn you it's pretty nasty in there."

She just looked at him and then disappeared down the hall.

Tom pulled out the chair at the desk and sat down. There were two drawers on the right side of the desk. The smaller top drawer was almost empty except for some old envelopes and a few hand tools. The larger bottom drawer had a rack with file folders in it. Tom started at the front and scanned the files. Nothing of note, just information on the property from the realtor which, to no surprise was Advantage Realty, Gary Shields' company. The other files contained correspondence from the town and the county relating to different taxes and fees. Nothing incriminating here, Tom thought. At least nothing that he was looking for.

Sherry appeared in the doorway and she looked angry.

"Fuckers," she said.

"What?"

"I got into the armoire."

"And?" Tom asked, prompting her.

"First of all, there's a hidden video camera on the top shelf," she began, the anger evident in her voice. "And worse than that there are some tools in there that would make the Marquis de Sade blush."

Tom thought for a second, still not what I'm looking for. "I told you these guys were bad." He pushed the file drawer closed and felt it stick a little. He pulled it open and closed it again, and again felt the resistance.

"I think there should be mandatory castration for freaks like that," Sherry went on.

Tom had pulled the top drawer open again and felt it also resist slightly. He lifted the front of the drawer and pulled it off the sliders all the way out. He turned it over on top of the desk, emptying the contents. An envelope had been taped to the bottom of the drawer and the tape was coming off one of the corners. Tom pulled the envelope the rest of the way off. It was addressed to Donna Shields at her Nottingham Terrace home. The postmark was four months old.

"What is that?" Sherry said, temporarily shelving her indignity.

"It could be the answer to a lot of things," Tom said thoughtfully.

Tom pushed the contents of the drawer back inside it and slid the drawer back into the desk. The seal on the envelope had already been broken and Tom pulled out the contents. There was an unlabeled DVD in a case and a piece of paper folded in half. Tom opened up the paper and revealed and hand drawn map. At the bottom of the map were two horizontal lines, probably indicating a road, with the word 'Stag' written between them. Then there was a line that ran up the center of the page to a fork. The right fork trailed off to nothing, as though the mapmaker had lost interest. The left fork ended at an oddly shaped blob. At about a quarter of the way around the right side of the blob was an X. Tom looked at the map for a moment. It didn't make a lot of sense. There explanation had to be on the DVD but there wasn't a computer on the desk or anything in the office to play it on. Tom placed the DVD and the map back in the envelope and stood up.

"Did you see a DVD player downstairs?" he said moving towards the door.

"Not that I noticed. But no real pervert should be without one."

They went down the stairs and looked all over the area where the fireplace was with the flat screen TV hanging over it. There had to be a closet somewhere with the electronics.

Tom checked is watch, it was 9:15. "Was there anything in the lounge?" he asked.

"I didn't see anything, just a couple of chairs and a massage table."

"Shit," Tom whispered. He briefly thought about putting the envelope back. No, he told himself, he had come too far. In his opinion Gary Shields and Mike Manzella were major scumbags and deserved whatever they got. He worried about his job briefly also but part of his mind told him that this was more important that being some low rent private dick. He tucked the envelope in his belt under his jacket.

"Let's get out of here," he said to Sherry.

He had expected her to protest about taking the envelope. “I’m right behind you,” she said.

They went over to the door. It was fully dark out now and as they stepped outside they were greeted by the sight of the grubby caretaker climbing onto the porch with a shotgun pointed towards them.

CHAPTER 14

The caretaker looked just as startled as Tom felt and almost lost his footing on the stairs. He caught his balance and then raised the shotgun and pointed it at Tom's head.

"Who the hell are you?" he asked.

Tom had stepped in front of Sherry and raised his hands.

"Are you crazy? Get that gun out of my face," Tom yelled.

"You tell me who you are first."

"I told you, I am a friend of Mike's and he is going to-"

"Bullshit," The caretaker interrupted and moved slightly forward. "I just talked to Donny and he said that there ain't no party tonight."

"Listen you idiot, when I talk to Mike you'll be awful sorry."

The old man snorted and sneered, "We'll see about that. I thought there was something funny going on so I went across the street and borrowed their phone. Donny and Mr. Manzella are on their way here right now."

"This is bullshit," Sherry said suddenly as she

stepped out from behind Tom.

Don't move! Neither one of ya!" the caretaker yelled.

Sherry held up her left arm in front of her face. "Don't! I just met this guy tonight," she yelled nodding at Tom. "He picked me up at the club. Said he was a friend of Gary's. I've got nothing to do with this!" She took a step to her left to distance herself from Tom.

"Shut up," the caretaker yelled. From the front house the dogs started barking. He pointed his weapon at Sherry.

"You miserable bitch," Tom yelled, turning on Sherry. "Why don't you shut your mouth?"

"I said shut up!" the old man turned the gun back at Tom.

In an instant Sherry brought her right hand up from her side and discharged a stream of pepper spray into the old man's eyes. He screamed and took a step back. Tom lunged forward grabbing the barrel of the gun with his left hand and following up with a blow to his jaw with his right hand. The caretaker went down in a heap with one hand still clinging to the rifle. Tom kicked the old man in the ribs hard and the pulled the gun away. The caretaker rolled down the steps and landed in a heap at the bottom. Up front the dogs were going crazy.

Tom dropped the shotgun over the railing into a nearby bush and said to Sherry, "We should go."

Sherry looked like she was all adrenaline. Pretty impressive, Tom would think to himself later.

"Monty! Duke!" the old man yelled as he was lying on his side with his fists rubbing in his eyes. What the hell was he yelling? In the distance came the distinct sound of cracking wood that sounded like a screen door being ripped off its hinges.

"Dogs!" Sherry yelled pointing towards the caretaker's house.

Tom looked up and saw two shadows approaching up the long driveway. One of the dogs was halfway there. The other dog seemed to be favoring a bad hind leg but seemed just as eager. Tom and Sherry ran to his car with Tom fumbling to get the keys out of his pocket. When he heard the sound of the dog's paws closing in on them on the gravel driveway he went to step in front of Sherry but she pushed him out of the way. The large black dog was less than five yards away when Sherry's gun went off and dropped him in mid stride.

He tumbled forward and let out a howl. The older limping dog stopped in its tracks still with twenty yards to go. Tom straightened up as Sherry stepped forward to the wounded animal.

"What did you do?" the old man screamed. He had sat up and was trying unsuccessfully to see what was going on.

Sherry stood over the dog that was bleeding heavily

from his shoulder. The animal's crying was getting quieter but it was still excruciating to listen to. She raised her gun and shot the dog in the head. The lame dog still stood motionless in the same spot. Sherry, not trusting it, backed towards the car. Tom unlocked the doors and they started to get in.

"No!" the caretaker yelled in a panicked voice. "What did you do to my dogs?"

Tom and Sherry drove off. Tom cut across Route Five and then turned north on Route Twenty. He knew he could probably drive right by Donny and Mike Manzella headed in the opposite direction but he didn't want to take a chance. He felt his heart rate getting back to normal and slowed the car down to a respectable 55 MPH.

"Nice going back there," Tom said. "But what are you doing with a gun in your purse?"

Sherry had pulled her hair back and was checking out the Sig Sauer 9 mm in her lap. She made sure the safety was back on and put the gun back in her bag.

"Don't worry. I have a carry permit."

"That's not what I meant. Why did you have it with you?"

Sherry wiped her forehead with the palm of her hand and looked over at Tom.

"I always carry it," Sherry said. "Kind of like a security blanket I guess. It's a dangerous world out there Donovan, especially for a girl who likes to stick her nose in other people's business."

That's some pretty sound logic, Tom thought.

He dropped Sherry off at her apartment with his sincere thanks. Before she got out of the car she told him that she better not be getting the brush off and made him promise to keep her informed on the case.

Tom got home at shortly after 10:15. He flipped on the lights and went over to the TV stand. He turned on the set and the DVD player then popped the disc in.

The screen went blue and then a video recording came on. There was a chair in front a drab tile wall. A tall skinny man with a brush cut and tattoos up and down his forearms came from behind the camera and sat in the chair. He looked tired and hungry. He had acne scars and a straggly goatee and was wearing an orange jumpsuit.

"Hi Donna," he said quietly with a sneer. "Surprised to see me? You probably thought you seen the last of 'ol Dillon huh? Well I borrowed this camera from the Chaplain. I told him I wanted to work on my speech to the parole board but I had something else in mind. Hell, the last hearing they told me I didn't have a chance at doin' less than ten years so why the fuck even bother, you know? Anyway, the reason you are looking at my pretty face is I need your help. And I ain't asking you I'm telling you." Here Dillon unfolded a piece of paper from his pocket. Tom recognized it immediately. "See this here is like a treasure map only there ain't no treasure by the x." He pointed his finger at the x and then looked back at the camera. "That is where you and me and your little sister dropped off your step-daddy, remember?"

Tom paused the playback and looked at the map. He could barely believe what he had just heard. The map told him nothing new so he hit play again.

Dillon sat forward and looked straight into the camera. He had dark piercing eyes. "All I need are three things. Number one: you and Mr. Moneybags are going to hire me a real lawyer," he began. "That dumb-assed public defender they assigned me didn't do shit for my case. After that I want you to get Angela to tell the DA that she lied about me and her daddy after we got busted. She has to say that the drugs were all the old man's and I had nothing to do with it. And third, I want twenty grand in cash when I get out. That's it, and then I disappear. I will miss Buffalo and knockin' boots with your sister but hey, live and let live I say." Dillon turned as if he heard someone at the door. "Okay, I gotta go. I'm sure I will be hearing from ya real soon Donna. If not my next phone call is going to be to the Sheriff's office. I think they still have a dive team."

Dillon stood up and walked directly in front of the camera and then the screen flashed back to blue.

"Holy crap," Tom said to himself. The Shields certainly had their fair share of skeletons. Now he understood why this package meant so much to Donna. Her half sister and her had something to do with her stepfather's disappearance a few years back and some convict was trying to use it as blackmail. He played the DVD again this time taking notes. Most of what he wrote down were questions. Who was Dillon? Was the stepfather involved in something illicit with this guy? He had referred to a relationship with Donna's half sister Angela, was that for real? He flipped back in his notes to a previous page checked something and then wrote down, "D. Stanton (step dad) disappears 2006," under the notes on Dillon.

He called Brian Dinkle's cell but it went to voicemail. He wanted to keep things moving, but he needed some research done first. He hadn't slept well for the last couple of nights and his head still hurt. He brushed his teeth got undressed and laid down in bed.

His phone buzzed. He felt like he had just gotten to sleep but the clock on his nightstand said it was 1:00 AM. He looked at the phone and checked the caller ID. He didn't recognize the number.

"Yeah," he said hoarsely.

"Tom Donovan?" The voice sounded vaguely familiar.

"Yeah. Who's this?"

"We met last night. How's the head?" It was Katrina.

"Listen, I am glad-"

"Hush, Donovan," she interrupted. "This is not a social call. I just wanted to make sure you gave our message to Gary and his friends."

"I didn't have to."

The line went quiet for a moment. Tom started to wonder if she had hung up.

"What are you talking about?" Katrina asked.

Tom took a guess now on something he hadn't thought about before he fell asleep. "I have the package that they were holding over Donna's head."

"You don't know what you are talking about."

"I have a pretty good idea," Tom said. "Before you knocked me out last night you were saying something about you and Donna having something that Shields and Manzella wanted back, and would trade it for something that they had. All I'm saying is I've got it."

"You're lying," Katrina hissed.

Tom thought for a second and said, "Okay then, I don't know anything about the drugs and Donna's missing stepfather and a guy named Dillon."

Katrina exhaled audibly and then went silent. Finally she said, "What do you want?"

"Excuse me?"

"Listen," she began. "I know I'm dealing with a fool, but let's cut to the chase. What's your angle?"

"I don't have an angle," Tom replied.

Katrina's voice betrayed a trace of impatience. "Then you're a bigger fool than I thought. I already told you what would happen if you and I cross paths again. Now your telling me that you double-crossed your employers. You must not know them too well because if you did you would know that you are as good as dead already."

"I'll take my chances," Tom told her.

"Oh yeah I forgot," she said. "I did a little research on you last night. "You're the Wyatt Earp of the McKinley Projects."

Bitch, Tom thought. "Not anymore. I do know that Manzella is just some wanna-be mobster and Shields is just a scam artist."

"That is a fair assessment," Katrina said. "But Manzella has some friends in Chicago and Toronto that he's trying to impress. You shouldn't underestimate him."

"Oh, I won't."

"So I will ask you again Mr. Donovan. What do you want for the package."

"Nothing," Tom said. "At least nothing like money"

"Really? I find that hard to believe since you are being paid by Gary Shields."

Tom chuckled in spite of himself. "I believe that milk has already soured."

"I'm not sure what that means and I don't care. And what do you want if you don't want money."

"I just want to hear Donna's side of the story," Tom said.

"What for?"

"For my own peace of mind I guess. I just want

to know that I did they right thing as I kiss another career goodbye."

"Hmm," Katrina paused, "We're going to have to talk about this. I'll call you tomorrow."

"Katrina wait-"

It was too late, the line went dead.

Tom tossed and turned for a few hours unable to get back to sleep. He really hadn't put it in perspective until he had just said it out loud to a stranger. He was probably done as a private investigator. Another bridge burned to the ground lay in his wake. It felt like a pattern had developed and was repeating itself. He finally drifted off into a fitful sleep.

Chapter 15

Tom awoke at 7:00 AM. He was still tired but his mind was racing. He put on his trainers and went out for a run but the fatigue and the pain on the side of his head made him cut it short.

When he got back to the apartment he checked his phone. He had missed a call from his Uncle Sam. He decided he would call him back later. He had too much on his mind. He took a shower, shaved and left for the office.

He got to the office shortly before nine. He sat in his car and looked down at the envelope on the seat next to him. He told himself it was too late now to turn back. Tom would finish what he started with or without Cal Frederickson's approval. The only thing he hoped was that he had a few more days with the agency's resources at his disposal.

As he entered the reception area he saw Grace's desk was unoccupied and Sherry coming out of Cal's office. A slight panic came over him. Had she gone to Cal and told him what happened at the farmhouse? Had Cal found out on his own somehow and now Sherry's job would be in jeopardy too? Sherry must have picked up on his distress because she gave a slight smile and held up a file folder.

"Back to work," she said. "Wayward husband to watch."

Relieved that she wasn't headed down the hall with a box to clean out her desk Tom regained his composure. "They say hell has no wrath."

"Donovan!" Cal yelled from inside his office.

Sherry winked at Tom and turned to go down the hall.

Tom stood in the doorway to Cal's office. "C'mon in and shut the door," Cal ordered.

Tom sat down and waited. Cal finished typing something into his computer and then sat back and looked up at him. He just sat looking impassively, as if he were waiting for Tom to start. Tom tried to show nothing and was wondering if he could pull it off.

"What's happening on the Shields thing?" Cal finally said.

Tom cleared his throat and said, "I actually spoke to her accomplice, or friend, or what ever you want to call her. Turns out they knew each other at school."

"What does her friend have to do with this?" Cal asked.

"She seems to be acting as Donna's bodyguard," Tom began. "Brian found out she was in the military, had some special forces training. She actually threatened me last night and I think she would back it up if she was cornered. Beyond that I'm not sure if her connection to the matter goes any deeper. I proposed a meeting with Donna and Gary to try to hash things out."

"What did she say?"

"She said they would call me back."

Cal looked down and rubbed his temple with his right hand. After he thought for a moment he said, "I guess that's all that Gary Shields asked for. What do you think the odds are that they will agree?"

Tom's stomach was tight and he realized it was because he was lying to a man who had taken a chance on him and entrusted him with an important case. He decided right then that it might help if he injected a little truth into his narrative. "Well, I think we might have a problem there."

Cal looked back up at him. "What kind of problem?"

"This woman, Katrina, claims that Showgirls Gentlemen's Club is into a lot more than harmless adult entertainment," he told Cal. "Some of the dancers are turning tricks for your old friend Mike Manzella. She also alluded to the fact that drugs are being sold out of the club."

Cal rocked back in his chair and exhaled. "I knew as soon as I heard his name that this kind of shit would be happening."

A moment went by and neither of them said anything. Cal seemed to be lost in thought. Tom really wanted to get out of there so he decided to break the silence.

"What do you want me to do?" Tom asked.

Cal thought for another moment and said, "Wait

and see if they call back. Let me think about this until they do. If Donna is afraid of her husband and Manzella then I don't think she'll go for a meeting and frankly I don't blame her. I got half a mind to call that Lieutenant Kruger from the Lackawana PD or the DEA and tell them what you just told me, but all we have is hearsay from an angry wife." He scratched his chin again. "Let me think. And when I call you answer your damned phone." As he said that he pointed a beefy index finger at Tom.

Tom stood up. "You got it boss."

Grace was back at her desk and looked up as Tom came out of Cal's office. She held up a message slip. "Tom, your uncle called twice," she said. "He said it's very important that you call him back as soon as possible."

"Thanks," Tom said as he took the slip and turned to go down the hall.

"He said it was urgent," she called after him.

Tom went into his office. Sherry was pulling on her coat getting ready to leave.

"So, every thing alright?" she asked.

"For now. How about you? Are you okay?"

"Well, my feet are a little sore from the heels I was wearing last night but yeah, I'm fine," she told him.

Tom smiled for a second and them became serious. "Sherry, thanks again for last night. I should have never put you in that spot."

She smiled back at him. "Hey, I haven't had that

much fun in a long time. As long as we don't make a habit of it."

"Hell no," Tom said. "But if I ever need another rabid dog taken out you'll be my first call."

"That is so sweet," she said. "I gotta go. Be careful, okay?

"I will. You too." And she was gone.

Tom pushed the door shut and looked at the message slip. His uncle wouldn't have called three times if it wasn't important. He punched the number in and hit send. The call went to voicemail. He looked up the number for D district and called it. He asked for Captain Dipietro and was put through after a couple of minutes.

"Uncle Sam, it's Tom"

"Oh, hey, can I call you right back?" his uncle said quickly.

Tom heard voices in the background. His uncle was not alone "Sure," he said and then Sam clicked off.

Tom took out his notebook and tore out a blank page. Then he opened up the book to the notes he had made last night. He started writing on the blank page:

First name- Dillon - Last name- ?.
Resided in Clarence or nearby.
Arrested 2005 -2006? Narcotics conviction?
Step father Dave Stanton- Arrest record?

He got up from his desk and went down the hall to Brian's office. He went in without knocking and found Brian with his feet up on his desk sound asleep.

"Hey, Rip Van Winkle," Tom said tapping Brian's foot.

Brian's eyes opened slowly and focused. "What?"

"I can see that you're buried here, but I was wondering if you could do a web search on these two guys?"

Brian sat up and rubbed at the corner of his right eye. He looked down at the sheet Tom handed him. Tom thought he looked disoriented. "Brian, you okay?"

"Yeah Tommy-boy," he responded. "Just doing a little meditation. Don't worry, I have already forgiven your intrusion into my Zen moment." He pulled his chair in front of his computer. "This is all pretty recent. Shouldn't be a problem."

Tom's phone buzzed. He recognized his uncle's number. "Thanks Brian. I'll be down the hall."

He left Brian to do his research and answered his phone. "Uncle Sam."

"We have to talk kid," Sam whispered and he sounded serious. "Can I meet you."

"Can it wait until tonight?" Tom asked.

"No, we should do it sooner."

Tom thought about Katrina and Donna. He wanted to make sure he was available if they decided to actually call him .

"Crap Sam, I am kind of up to my neck in something. What is it?"

Over the phone Tom heard a car door slam. His uncle had obviously left his office to make the call.

Sam exhaled and said, "Is there something you want to tell me?"

Tom bristled slightly. "Tell you about what?"

"About you, Joe Walczak and Derrick Trent?"

"What the hell are you talking about?" Tom asked and his voice was rising.

"I was at a meeting downtown last night, and after the meeting few of us went out for a drink. Do you remember Phil Sestak from Narcotics?"

"Yeah."

"Well, Sestak corners me last night," Sam continued. "And he has a pretty good load on. He starts talking about how you had better watch out because he thinks you might have a problem with this lawsuit."

"What kind of problem?" Tom asked.

"Right before the shooting he said that they were putting together a task force with the DEA. Sestak said he had the feeling at the time that the whole thing was a way for the DEA to get information on Buffalo Cops. Sestak claimed the DEA guys did everything but ask if there were dirty cops in E district. Sestak and his boss started getting a little suspicious."

"There was never a task force?" Tom asked.

"It never got off the ground," Sam answered. "Sestak said the DEA guys didn't trust them and they were being all secretive. It came down from the commissioner's office that we wouldn't work in the dark. Sestak said the whole situation kind of went away when Derrick Trent died."

Tom felt his face get hot. He felt like throwing his phone at the wall. He knew he had to keep his temper in check. Things were happening behind the scenes and it made him anxious.

"Tom, are you there?" His uncle brought him back to the present.

"Yeah, just thinking. Listen Uncle Sam, you have to believe me when I tell you that you know absolutely everything about me and Derrick Trent. I fucked up and got my partner crippled for life but that's it. There was no ulterior motive for shooting Trent."

Sam exhaled again. "I though so Tom. I know it's bullshit but I just wanted to hear you say it. But this might get ugly if the DEA agents testify against you."

"Did Sestak say who his contacts at the DEA were?" Tom asked.

"Why do you need to know that?" Sam said. "You aren't going to do something stupid are you?"

"No. I was just wondering if it's anybody I crossed paths with. Maybe somebody has a hard-on for me."

Sam thought for a moment. "He mentioned one

name, the agent in charge. I think it was Wilson. But he did mention another guy who was with Wilson and seemed to be the one trying to dig stuff up. Sestak didn't remember his name but he said it was some big guy with a shaved head."

That would probably be Agent Dan Casey. The same Agent Casey was who had pointed an assault rifle in Tom's face on that night two years ago.

"Any of that sound familiar?" Sam asked.

Tom hesitated for a moment as if he were thinking and said "No, not really."

He told his uncle he would call Stanely the lawyer and share this information with him. He also told him that he would leave his uncle's name out of it. Sam told him not to worry about that and to watch his back. Sam also made Tom promise not to be such a shit and take his calls in the future.

Tom logged onto his computer and looked up information on the local DEA office while he thought about his next move.

Brian knocked and walked in. He was looking at one of the pages he had just printed out. "Nice crowd you been running with lately Mr. Donovan."

"What do you have?" Tom asked.

"For starters Dillon's last name is Jankowski. Or I should say was Jankowski."

"He's dead?" Tom asked and looked up at Brian.

"Extremely. He was doing a ten-year sentence for

narcotics possession with intent to distribute. It was his second trip upstate so they threw the book at him. He met his untimely demise when he got shanked during a fight in the dining hall last month." Brian flipped the page. "The guy who shanked him was some bad-ass from New York City already doing a life sentence for beating a junkie to death in '05."

"Anything on Stanton, the stepfather?"

Brian flipped to the last page. "Not a lot except he was into the IRS and the state of New York for about a two hundred grand when he closed up his car dealership."

Tom thought about it. Dillon Jankowski and Dave Stanton had been selling drugs together and then Stanton disappears. Jankowski takes over and, not being the brightest bulb, gets himself arrested. Was Donna's half sister part of their operation? Tom flipped back a few pages in his book to his notes on Angela, the stepsister. Her arrest as a minor would have been around the same time as Dillon Jankowki's.

Was Jankowski's claim true? Did something happen with Stanton that convinced his step daughter and daughter that the best thing to do was to stash his body? And then Dillon tries to blackmail Donna Shields. Did Gary Shields intervene? Tom wondered if Shields was desperate enough to reach out to his business partner, Mike Manzella, to help him get rid of Jankowksi. Tom realized he didn't have enough and now was just speculating.

Tom looked up and Brian was staring at him. "Major Tom, welcome back."

"Sorry, Brian. Thanks. Good stuff as always."

"Anything else?" Brian asked.

"Yeah, there is," Tom said and he picked up the envelope from the desk and took out the hand drawn map. "Look at this and tell me if you see anything."

Brian took the map and studied it. Without saying anything he went over to Sherry's desk, sat down at her computer, and logged on. Tom was pretty sure Sherry had her own password but didn't want to interrupt. Tom stood up and went over to watch. Brian opened up a map program and typed in a few words. After he zoomed in to what he wanted he sat back and said put his finger on the screen on the image of a body of water and said "I'm thinkin' that this be where your treasure be buried captain."

"How do you know?" Tom asked, politely smiling at Brian's pirate impersonation.

"The bottom of the page the word Stag is either a misspelling or shorthand for Stage Road." Brian pointed to a line on the top of the monitor that said "Stage Road." Then he turned the paper map upside down and held it up next to the screen. Tom saw it then. The computer image depicted a cemetery with a large lake in it. The lines on the paper map coincided with the narrow paths that went through the cemetery, one going past the lake and one leading right to it. The blob Jankowski had drawn represented the lake.

"Where is this place?" Tom asked gesturing towards the screen.

"Clarence. I've actually been in that cemetery."

"Do you have family there?"

"No. Doing a little ghost hunting," Brian said and smiled sheepishly.

Tom nodded. "Of course. I should have guessed."

Brian stood up and looked at Tom flatly. "It's a great way to meet women."

"I didn't know that either. Thanks Brian. I owe you big for all this stuff."

"No worries, Major Tom. You just keep those fees rolling into the agency."

"I'll do my best," Tom said and grabbed his jacket and was headed for the door.

Chapter 16

Tom had to make three stops before he found a payphone. He knew the public telephone was an endangered species, but he hadn't realized that they were so close to becoming completely extinct. He finally found a bank of phones at the bus station on Division Street, picked the phone that looked the least likely to be germ infested, deposited his money and punched in the number. After wading through the automated answering service he got to the right office.

"Federal Building, Drug Enforcement. How may I direct your call?"

Tom lowered his voice, "Agent Casey, please."

"Who's calling please?"

"Tell him it's a former friend of Derrick Trent."

"Please hold."

The line went quiet. Several minutes passed and Tom was prompted to put more money in twice. A slight wave of paranoia came over him and he wondered if they were already trying to trace the call.

"This is Casey," a voice said.

"Agent Casey I think I have something you may be

interested in," Tom said.

"Who is this?"

"Take it easy, slick. You really need to see what I have."

Casey was becoming irritated. "Listen. asshole, I don't have time for your bullshit. What do you know about Derrick Trent?"

Jackpot, Tom thought. Either the Trent matter was still open or it was a sore spot for Casey.

"Ah, I knew that name would get your attention," Tom said. "What I have will blow your mind."

"Okay, so bring it in," Casey said.

Tom laughed. "Are you kidding me? I am not coming within a mile of that place. No, you come to me."

"Fuck you, pal. Do you think I'm stupid? You couldn't possibly have anything I would need that badly."

Tom hesitated and then said, "You're not even interested in the cops who killed him and your buddy?"

Now Casey paused. Tom could hear him breathing. "Let's say I'm interested. What do you want?"

"Nothing," Tom said.

"Nothing?"

"Let's just say that it's something I need to get off my chest as a law abiding citizen."

Casey's voice dropped into a growl. "Listen punk, this better be on the level or I am going to forget I am a federal officer and kick the living shit out of you."

"I'll take my chances," Tom responded. "Meet me in a half hour at the Naval Park. I'll be on a bench near the bow of The Sullivans. Oh, and I give it to you and you only."

"Wait a second-" Casey started to say as Tom slammed the phone down.

Twenty minutes later Tom parked his car in the lot off of Marine Drive. It was a sunny day, but there was a cold wind coming off the lake. He went to his trunk and grabbed a hooded sweatshirt out of his gym bag and put it on with the hood up under his jacket.

The park was almost deserted. The few people there were moving briskly, probably due to the frigid wind. Tom headed to the benches that looked out over the three decommissioned warships that made up the naval museum. None of the benches were occupied so Tom took the one closest to the bow of the USS The Sullivans.

The ship had been named for the five Sullivan brothers who died in the Battle of the Solomon Islands during World War II when their ship went down. It was shortly after that the navy decided to prohibit brothers from serving on the same vessel.

His phone buzzed in his pocket. He had the sensation he was being watched so he left it there. After about ten more minutes Tom spotted a figure coming from his right. He didn't want to look up until he was sure. The figure stopped in front of him and Tom looked up. Casey's face darkened as soon as he recognized him.

"What the fuck are you doing here?" Casey sputtered.

In the distance Tom thought he heard tires squeal.

"We have to talk," Tom said.

"I've got nothing to say to you."

"I don't know what you think you know, but I'm not dirty."

Just then Tom heard a engine race up behind him and then brakes and rubber squealing as a vehicle came to a stop. He turned his head and saw two men hopping out of a black SUV with their hands reaching inside there coats. He turned to Casey who had his hand up stopping the two other agents from coming any closer.

"You better not be armed."

Tom stood up and slowly took off his jacket and hoodie. He laid them on the bench and turned around. The two agents by the truck looked edgy. He turned all the way around and looked at Casey. Casey nodded to the other agents and Tom heard the trucks doors slam and then the vehicle drove off.

Casey frowned. Tom put his sweatshirt and jacket back on.

"Let's just say it got back to me that you had a hard-on for me even before I shot Trent," Tom said.

Casey smiled but without any humor behind it. "Who told you that, your Uncle Sammy?"

Tom shook his head. "Guess again."

"Then it had to be that fat old drunk Sestak."

"Nope."

"Look, I don't have the time or the inclination to burn anybody down for having a big mouth. I just want to know who I can trust over at police headquarters."

Tom thought about it for a moment and said, "You know I still have dreams about that night all the time. I don't give a rat's ass about Trent, but I will never get over killing Carl."

The top of Casey's head turned a little red and Tom thought he might have dredged up something that he shouldn't have. Casey took his time and was obviously trying calm himself. Finally he said, "First of all, you are pissing me off just mentioning Carl. He was a good man and a good agent. Secondly, you never answered my question. What makes you think we are looking at you? What brings you here after two years, pulling a bullshit stunt like this?"

Tom looked at Casey trying to get a reading on him. "Have you received a summons from Derrick Trent's family?"

"Yes."

Great, Tom thought, one-word answers. "Whatever Trent told you people about me is bullshit. He was just trying to save his own ass and take a few of us down with him."

Casey shook his head and smiled wryly. "You got

old Derrick all wrong," he said.

"What are you talking about?"

"He said that you were a real boy scout. He would've never approached you."

"So what do the lawyers want from you?" Tom asked.

"I'll give you a second to figure that out," Casey responded.

Tom frowned trying to figure out what Casey was saying. Then it hit him.

"No fucking way!"

"You didn't hear it from me."

"Joe Walczak? That's crazy!"

"It's a crazy world Donovan." Casey started to turn to leave.

"I was his partner. I would have known," Tom said.

Casey looked back over his shoulder. "Did you know that your own Internal Affairs people had a file on him? Yeah, but I guess they felt bad for him after being put in a wheelchair and all, so they shelved it."

"Bullshit."

"Hey, you don't believe me ask your uncle. He's got a big fucking mouth. He'll tell you."

Tom wanted to run after Casey and punch him in the head but he found himself weighed down, out of breath and confused. How much of any of it was true? It would be a good half hour before Tom got up off the bench. He didn't even notice the cold.

CHAPTER 17

Tom finally stirred himself and walked back to the parking lot. His head was spinning and he felt nauseous. He climbed into his car and put the key into the ignition but didn't start the engine.

He tried to think of what to do next. If what Casey had alluded to was true, how had he missed it? He had been partnered with Joe Walczak for over two years. You get to a point where you think you know most everything about somebody after that long. *Almost everything*, that was the key phrase. Growing up in the environment Tom had as well as being a cop for ten years he knew that people always kept secrets.

He could call his uncle. No, he thought, Sam had called him because he was concerned that Tom was under some kind of cloud. Casey had dispelled that, to a point. He had to talk to Joe; lawyers be damned. Despite the fact that Casey had said what he did he still had to give his old partner a chance to explain.

He pulled his phone out and looked at the screen. He had totally forgotten that it had buzzed while he was waiting on the bench. No voice mail just a number on the caller ID he didn't recognize. He remembered the morning and avoiding his uncle's call and its importance so he pressed the send button.

"Mr. Donovan?"

It was a voice Tom thought he knew but couldn't be sure.

"Speaking. Who's this?"

"Mr. Donovan this is Donna Shields."

Tom collected his thoughts and tried to focus. "Hello, Donna."

"Is it true what you told Katrina? That you have the DVD and the map?"

"Yes, I have them."

"How did you get them?"

"That's kind of a long story. Let's just say I got them without the consent of your husband or his partner."

Donna hesitated for a moment and then said, "And you don't want anything for them?"

"Not really. I just want to clear a few things up."

"What kind of things?" she asked.

Tom checked his watch it was 2:35 PM. "Like I told Katrina, I just want a little information that's all. Nothing incriminating, I just want to get a feel for your husband and Manzella. Then I give you the envelope and you and Katrina can disappear."

Donna sighed heavily. "You know Katrina doesn't trust you. As a matter of fact she probably would have killed you the other night if we would have been anywhere else."

"It's good to have somebody watching your back I guess," Tom said. "But she seems to have a little bit of a violent streak."

Tom thought he heard Donna laugh ever so quietly. "She is excitable."

They were quiet for a moment and then Tom came back, "I'll tell you what. I'll give you the envelope and just ask a few questions. If there is anything you don't want to answer just say so and I leave. No strings attached."

"Hold on," Donna said. Then it sounded like she muffled the phone and Tom could hear her speaking to someone in the background, probably Katrina.

"Can you be out on Transit Road in Williamsville by six o'clock?"

"Yeah, where on Transit?"

"Just be in the area. Trina will call you at six and give you the address."

Tom thought for a moment. This was probably non negotiable. "I'll be there."

He heard Katrina in the background again and then Donna said, "Oh, and don't bother calling this number again. We're getting rid of this phone." Before Tom could respond the line went dead.

Tom thought about going back to the office but didn't want to get into another prolonged conversation with

Cal. He thought he had given his boss just about as much information as he could have without getting himself in trouble. After he was done with the Shields he was pretty sure all would be revealed anyway and then he would just have to sit back and accept the consequences.

He thought about Joe. He had gotten such a weird vibe from Joe when he was at this house on Tuesday. Part of him wanted to believe that there was no way in hell that Joe had done something shady that had anything at all to do with the death of Derrick Trent. He was also starting to get the sick feeling in his stomach you get when you realize somebody you trusted has lied to you. He pulled out his phone and punched in Joe's number. After four rings the answering machine picked up. Tom clicked off.

He was back at his apartment and had a few hours to kill. He flipped through his notebook and then put it aside. He felt restless so he stripped down to his t-shirt and shorts and headed to the spare room where he had a speed bag mounted. He didn't use the bag that often because the lady downstairs politely mentioned that it was right over her son's bedroom and it would wake him up if Tom used it too early in the morning or late at night. Tom worked the bag for about thirty minutes, working up a pretty good sweat and relieving at least a little bit of the tension from the afternoon. He jumped in the shower and then walked to his bedroom.

As he was getting a fresh shirt out of his closet he

looked up at the shelf. He reached up and pushed aside an accordion file that held some personal papers in it and took out a shoe box that was behind it. He took the box out to the kitchen and opened it on the table. Inside the box was and unregistered Smith and Wesson .38 caliber revolver that had belonged to his father. Tom unwrapped the gun from the cloth that was around it and set it down on the newspaper he had left on the table.

Tom remembered finding the gun in a toolbox shortly after his father's death. His mother had finally agreed to sell the house on Hubbell Ave after she realized there were too many painful memories there. That's when Tom had started getting into trouble at school and in the neighborhood. Tom was assigned to clean out the basement and during the course of that he found the gun. He was pretty sure that few people knew of its existence, his mother in particular; so he decided to keep it from her. He smuggled the gun up to his room and stashed it in his gym bag under his boxing gear.

He had kept the gun in good working order through the years for some vague reason. He checked it cleaned it and even fired it a handful of times at Whitey Brennan's hunting cabin in Allegheny County. Whitey had seen the gun and asked Tom where he got it. Tom said it had been his Dad's and Whitey never pushed the issue. As a cop Tom had preferred his service weapon to his father's gun. The Glock 21 9mm he had carried on duty was lighter, carried more rounds and worked in all kinds of weather. But the Glock went with the badge and his legal right to carry a concealed weapon, and they were all things of the past. Tom had applied for a citizen's pistol permit, but the approval was still pending.

He took out the oil from under his sink and took the gun apart cleaned it, reassembled it and checked the sight. He looked into the box and saw the box of shells that he had purchased and few years ago. He took the box out and opened it.

He still sometimes missed the sense of security he felt from the weight of the Glock on his hip. Over the last two years he found himself feeling for it with his hand less and less. The last few days had been rather harrowing though and he wondered if he should bring the .38 with him. After about ten minutes Tom removed the bullets from the gun, wrapped it and put it back in the shoe box, then back on the shelf in the closet.

He took the slow rout up Main Street to Williamsville and got there shortly after 5:30 PM. He stopped and got gas and a large black coffee and parked his car in a half empty strip mall. He tried Joe's number and got the answering machine again, this time leaving a message to please call him back. Now he just had to wait for the call from Donna Shields.

At 6:05 his phone buzzed. The caller ID said restricted.

"Donovan," Tom said.

"Where are you?" It was Katrina.

"At a mini-mart near the mall."

"Alright, drive North on Transit about seven miles. Pull into the lot at the Stay-More Motor Lodge." She was all business.

"Which room are you in?"

"We'll tell you when you get here," Katrina said. "Just park away from any other cars."

"Got it," Tom said and she was gone.

Fifteen minutes later Tom pulled into the lot at the Save-More. He had no problem following Katrina's instruction regarding finding a wide-open space. There were only three other cars in the parking lot in the middle of the single story horseshoe shaped building. None of them was the white sedan Tom seen the two women in before, but that was no surprise. The Save-More had seen better days and looked to be on the verge of going out of business at first glance. Tom parked in the space he thought would be the most visible.

He glanced in the mirrors and through the windshield trying to figure out which rooms might be occupied, but saw nothing that looked like a sign of life.

Five minutes later a door opened towards the back of the building and a small dark haired woman stood and waited until she was sure she had his attention. After Tom made eye contact the woman shut the door. Tom grabbed the envelope off the passenger seat and climbed out of his car.

He knocked on the door and it opened. Donna Shields was standing by the bathroom door of the small unit and the door shut as soon as Tom stepped inside. Out of the corner of his eye he saw that it had been Katrina who closed the door and now once again she was pointing a handgun at his head, this time with a silencer attached.

"Turn around," she said after she had grabbed the envelope from him and tossed it on the bed. "Put your hands on the door."

Tom did as he was told and felt her pat him down with her left hand while her right was pointing the gun at the base of his skull. He heard Donna over by the bed now going through the envelope.

Tom, still facing the door with his hands up said over his shoulder. "Is it true? What Dillon said on the video?"

"Shut up," Katrina hissed, pressing the barrel of the gun harder into Tom's neck.

"Just a second," Donna said. "I'm going to check the disc."

Tom felt the pressure of the gun let up and then leave completely.

"Turn around," Katrina said.

Katrina had taken two steps back and seemed to be studying Tom. She had lowered the pistol to her side but

Tom had no doubt that she wouldn't hesitate to bring it up again if she felt he was a threat.

It was the first time he had actually seen her up close. She was about 5'5" and looked to be on the thin side. Tom knew from firsthand experience though that the dark clothes she had on probably concealed the fact that she was a lot stronger and tougher than her outward appearance suggested. She had brown hair that was pulled back in a ponytail and brown eyes that could be considered pretty, but had a certain world-weariness to them.

Katrina gave a little smile and said, "How's the head?"

Tom shrugged. "Alright, I guess. Although in the old days and under different circumstances I would definitely splash your nose all over your face."

"Oh, what's the matter Macho Man, don't you hit ladies?"

"Not usually, but I'd hit you in a heartbeat," Tom said.

"I would love to give you the chance to rescue your wounded pride," she said. "Or just finish the job I started."

"Trina, knock it off," Donna said from the bed where she had put the DVD into a laptop.

Donna turned the volume up and Tom could hear the voice of Dillon Jankowski explain his plan for getting out of jail again. After a few minutes she stopped the playback and slammed the computer shut. "Bastard!" She said.

"Dead bastard," Tom said. His comment drew a reproachful look from Katrina.

"What do you mean?" Donna asked looking up.

"You mean you," Tom began and then stopped. Suddenly it occurred to him to ask a question that he hadn't thought of before. "Is this the first time you've seen the video?"

Donna grimaced and said, "I didn't even know it existed before last week."

"Did Gary have it?"

"He told me he opened it and took it to his partner, Mike Manzella, to see if he could do anything about it," her voice trailed off.

"So how did you find out about it?" Tom asked.

Donna looked like she might be starting to cry. "I'd found some things out about the club recently. Bad things I didn't want to be involved in. I told Gary I was going to go to the police if he didn't make them stop."

"What did Gary say to that?"

"He said that he couldn't get out," she said. "He was afraid of Manzella. I told him that we could get a lawyer and claim that we knew nothing about it. I insisted that we go to the police. Then he changed...he got angry and told me about the package they had from Dillon." Tom waited while Donna tried to collect herself. "He said that they would use it if they had to and people would get hurt. Me, my sister..."

"So you left?"

"That was my idea," Katrina chimed in. "I always had my suspicions about Gary." She looked sympathetically towards Donna "He had a line of B.S. a mile long about how he was just some kid from humble origins chasing the American dream. I had him figured for a con man and a crook. I'm a lot more cynical than Donna."

A tear rolled down Donna's cheek. "The night I left I realized that Gary knew exactly what was going on. He was so angry and paranoid... I was scared enough to run."

The room was quiet for a moment and Tom finally asked, "So what about your step father? Is his body really in that lake."

"Yes," Donna said wiping her cheek with the back of her hand. "I killed him."

"Donna, that's enough," Katrina said. She turned towards Tom and said, "You'd better go."

"No Trina. He should hear this." She looked at Tom and her countenance seemed to shift from fear to anger. "Angela called me one night hysterical and said she had been raped. When I got to the house she told me that Dave Stanton, her own father, had brought that piece of shit Dillon to the house and that Dillon drugged her and had sex with her. She told me that since my stepfather had closed his car lot he and Dillon were selling crystal meth out of the house. She also told me that he was out of control and had been hitting her. When my stepfather came in I confronted him and he got angry. We were screaming at each other and he slapped me. Angela jumped on his back and he threw her on the ground and started kicking her."

Donna's eyes seemed to lose focus but she went on. "I grabbed the fireplace poker and hit him across the back of the head with it. He went down and I should have stopped...but I didn't. I don't know how many times I hit him, but when I finally stopped Angela was in the corner and it looked like she was in shock."

"And where does Dillon come in?" Tom asked.

"Turns out he had been outside waiting for my step-father and heard the whole thing. I don't know why he didn't come in while it was going on except maybe he wanted to see how things worked out. At first when I saw him I wanted to kill him too, but I kept thinking about Angela. We realized that we all had a lot to lose so we came to an agreement. We cleaned up the living room and dumped the body. My only condition was that Dilllon get all the drugs out of the house and leave my sister alone."

"And he agreed to that?"

"Yes, the greedy bastard figured he would run the business by himself, but he pissed somebody off and they informed on him. The Sheriff raided the house before he moved the drugs and arrested my sister. She swore a statement out about Dillon and she was released on probation. He was a repeat offender so he got sent to prison. He must have figured this was his best chance to get out."

Tom thought about the story for a moment. The room was quiet and he figured he had heard enough. "So now what?" he asked.

Donna sighed and stood up, straightening her blouse, "I'll be alright, but I'm worried about my sister and her family." She looked at Katrina. "We were thinking about giving the notebook I took from the safe at the club back as a peace offering and then getting out of town."

"I take it the notebook is a record of what's really going on at the club?"

"Yes," she answered.

"Do you think that Gary and Manzella will go for that?"

Katrina spoke again, "If they can't find Donna she will always be a threat. If something happens to Angela, her husband or her little girl we will come back and make Gary's life hell."

"If you decide to give it back I'd like to be there," Tom said.

"Why?" Katrina asked.

"Consider me insurance. If something goes wrong I may be able to help."

"I don't think so," Katrina said frowning.

"I don't get it Mr. Donovan," Donna interrupted. "You said my husband hired you and you don't seem to be acting in his interest at all."

"He and I have different interests," Tom said.

Katrina looked at Donna and then back at Tom. Then she gestured to the door.

"We'll see," she said. "Oh, and here." She took Tom's wallet off the dresser and tossed it to him. "You can have that back."

"Thanks," Tom said and left.

CHAPTER 18

Tom was driving South on Transit Road thinking about the fastest route back to the city when he found himself once again turning down Sheridan Drive heading in the direction of Joe Walczak's house. It was 8:45 when he looked at his phone. He pulled up Joe's number and hit send.

The answering machine again. After the beep Tom said, "Joe if you're home please pick up. We have to talk."

"Tommy?" Joe came on. His voice was thick. He sounded like he'd been drinking.

"Joe, we gotta talk. Something is going on and I need to ask you a few things."

"C'mon over, Tom. Lisa took Tyler over to her mom's for the night. The front door is open, walk right in."

Tom hadn't been expecting that. He recovered and said, "I'll be there in ten minutes."

The sun had almost set when he pulled in the driveway. The house was dark as far as Tom could see. He knocked on the door and pushed it open.

"Joe! It's Tom. Where are you?"

"In the office," Joe's voice called out. "Come on

back."

Tom walked in to Joe's makeshift office and found Joe seated behind his desk. He looked even more haggard than he had a few days ago. His eyes were bloodshot and Tom was convinced he was drunk.

"Joe, what the fuck is going on?"

"Easy Tommy. I can explain everything. But first I want you to read this." He pushed a piece of paper over the desk towards Tom.

Tom looked at the letter and read it under the light from the lamp on Joe's desk. The letter was a confession. It stated that Joe had gone to the projects on the night two years before with the intention of killing Derrick Trent. His plan was to use the beating of Alicia Simmons as a cover for confronting Trent. It stated that he had taken several payoffs from Trent in return for information on some of the NBH gang's competition. When the shooting happened he thought he would let nature take its course, but now he knew that he would be held accountable and wanted to clear the air. In the last paragraph he wrote that his partner, Tom Donovan, had never been a part of, or had any knowledge of his arrangement with Derrick Trent. He couldn't let his friend and ex-partner take the blame for something that was ultimately his fault.

Tom looked up at Joe and his red-rimmed eyes. "Jesus, Joe. Why?"

Joe broke eye contact with Tom. "Lisa was pregnant

and she was having a tough time," he began, his voice quiet. "She got laid off and they cancelled her insurance. That and I was two months behind on the mortgage."

"You should have said something."

"I thought about it Tom, I did," Joe said as he looked up at Tom. "But one night I was moonlighting, working the door at one of the clubs downtown and who should walk up to me but fucking Derrick Trent. He starts in about why would I need to take a second job with what I make as a cop? At first I am getting pretty pissed and thinking about punching his lights out. But then he makes me an offer. At first I tell him to fuck himself, but after a while he pulls out five hundred bucks and says that all he wants is some information on the Street Kings."

"You didn't?" Tom asked but he already knew the answer.

"Not until he put it in perspective."

"Perspective? What are you talking about?"

Joe looked away again when he said, "He told me as far as the Street Kings were concerned he and I were after the same thing, eliminating them. We could help each other in that way."

Tom wanted to hit him, to hit something but replied, "Joe, this is Derrick Trent we are talking about! Not some community watch captain!"

Joe forced himself to look back up at Tom. "I know that Tommy. But the bills were piling up and the bank was calling about the mortgage. Plus I was a little drunk and pissed off at the world that night. I lost my head."

Tom plopped down on a chair across from Joe. "How much did you give him?"

"I only met with him twice after that and only gave him intel we had on the Kings."

"How much did he pay you?" Tom asked, his fists clenched.

"$1200 all told. After that I told him we were through," Joe muttered.

Tom just stared at him. He looked beaten, a shadow of the man he had worked with and trusted; former high school football star, decorated cop. He had sold his soul for twelve hundred dollars.

"You should have told me. We could have figured something out."

Joe shook his head. "No, Tommy. Even though it was your gun that fired the shot, I always felt like I was the one who pulled the trigger. Hell, I almost did."

"What do you mean?" Tom asked.

Joe now looked directly at him, "The only reason the DEA guy went for his gun was I already had mine out."

"Shit."

Joe shook his head again and bit his lower lip. "Besides it's too late," he said. "I already mailed a copy of this letter to my lawyer, the judge and IAD this morning."

"What?"

Joe put a hand up and said, "The lawsuit Tom. Trent's Family and that vulture Mason are looking for a pound of flesh and I can't let you get fucked over again. Not only that, but I think Trent may have ratted me out to the DEA before he went down."

Tom fell silent. He was trying to think of some way, any way to make this all go away. Joe finally brought him back.

"Tom?" Joe whispered.

"Yeah."

"I just polished off a half bottle of whiskey and my mouth is dry as hell. Could you go to the kitchen and get me a glass of water?"

Tom hesitated for a moment.

"Please, Tom?" Joe asked, his eyes beseeching. "I want to try to sober up before Lisa gets home."

Tom went out to the kitchen and was filling a glass of water up at the sink when he remembered something. Hadn't Joe said Lisa and his son were staying the night at her mother's? He put the glass down on the sink board and hurried back to the office.

When he got back in he found Joe had wheeled himself from around the desk. He had a gun his right hand.

"What the fuck are you doing?" He took a step towards his friend.

"Stop right there," Joe said pointing the gun at Tom.

Tom froze and put his hands halfway up, "Joe,

don't do this, think about it." There was more to say but Tom couldn't think of the words.

Joe smirked a little and said, "I am. I'm glad your here Tom. It's one last thing off my mind."

"I don't understand," Tom said.

"Don't let Lisa see me like this," Joe said and the smirk faded. Then he put the gun his mouth and blew out the back of his skull.

Tom stood motionless for a moment with his ears ringing and the smoke clearing. He went over to Joe and felt his neck. His pulse was fading fast. He took his phone out and dialed 911.

In less than five minutes a patrol car pulled up in front of the Walczak's home. Tom had barely made it out the front door when the young patrolman was walking up the drive. The cop was young but poised.

"Are you the one who called 911?"

"Yeah," Tom answered, his voice calm. "My friend just shot himself in a room off the hall inside the house."

The young patrolman keyed the mike on his shoulder and was calling something in when another police car pulled up. A slightly older cop came up the drive and said, "Where is he?"

The first cop pointed towards the front door and said, "Room off the hall." The second cop hustled inside. Then the young cop, who had never really taken his eyes off Tom, said, "What's your name, sir?"

"Tom Donovan."

"And the man inside is a friend of yours you said?"

"Yeah, he was."

Then an EMT truck rolled up the young cop directed the crew inside the house.

"Let's go inside, sir. The detectives will need a statement."

"Right."

The young cop and Tom went into the kitchen. They could hear medics working although seemingly without a lot of urgency as he was pretty sure Joe had died almost instantly. Finally a middle-aged man in a coat and tie came into the kitchen.

"Do you know where Mr. Walczak's wife and son are?" he asked Tom.

"She's at her mother's house. Her name is Helen Carpenter. I think she lives in Getzville."

The detective looked at the patrolman and said, "Tell Detective Gates that, will you?"

The detective considered Tom for a moment and said, "Were you good friends with Mr. Walczak?"

"Did you know he used to be a cop?" Tom asked evenly.

"I did. I met him at a benefit dinner a year ago. Is that how you knew him?"

Tom noticed the detective was using the past tense

in his questions. "I was his partner," Tom said. "I was with him the night he got shot."

The detective's eyes widened almost imperceptibly. He shook his head. "Yeah, his poor wife." He looked back at Tom. "I know this is hard, but you understand, as clear cut as this looks I still need you to come in and make a statement."

"I understand," Tom said nodding. "Is your partner going to notify his wife?"

"Yeah, as soon as we get the address."

Tom thought about a message he might send, or even requesting to ride along to help break the news to Lisa. He knew the Amherst cops would never allow that and even if they did he wouldn't know what to say.

Tom was at the police station for the next three hours. When they allowed him to use the phone he called Bob Stanley's answering service and left a message. The detective he met at the house, whose name was Anderson, took Tom's statement in a professional, neutral tone. He asked Tom why he was at the house to which Tom replied with full disclosure that he went there to discuss the civil suit. He mentioned the letter that Anderson had collected from the scene and said that Joe had already mailed out several copies earlier to the judge and his attorney.

It occurred to Tom that a suspicious mind might develop the theory that he had gone there to coerce Joe into confessing, but the letters would have been post marked earlier than the 911 call. Actually there had been another call a minute later from a neighbor who had reported he heard a "loud bang" from Joe's house. Also, the physical evidence would prove that the gun was in Joe's hand when it went off. To remove any doubt Detective Anderson had Tom's hands tested for gunpowder residue.

As Anderson was escorting Tom out of the interview room Tom asked if his partner was back. Anderson led him to a desk where a balding man in his mid thirties was typing something into a computer.

"Detective Gates," Anderson said.

Gates looked up at Anderson and then Tom.

"Detective Gates, this is Tom Donovan. He's the one who called it in."

Gates stood up and offered his hand to Tom. "Sorry about your friend."

Tom thanked him and said, "Did you notify the widow?"

Gates nodded. "Yeah she was pretty shook up at first, but then told me that he had been depressed lately. We offered to stay, but she said no. She was going to have a cup of coffee with her mother and try to figure out how to explain it to her kid."

Tom nodded and looked down. The shock was starting to wear off and he felt like bawling his eyes out. Anderson put his hand on his arm and said, "Come on, I'll give you a ride to your car."

Tom sat in silence in the passenger seat all the way back to Joe's house. A Crime scene unit and a patrol car were still parked out front. There was yellow tape across the front door and a patrolman standing outside.

Anderson pulled up alongside Tom's car and looked over at him. Tom looked back and could tell Anderson had something on his mind.

"What is it, Detective?"

"I feel like a total shit for asking you but," he began.

"What is it? Go ahead."

Anderson sighed and gave a brief nod. "Tomorrow I am going to be in the chief's office and the first thing he is going to ask me is if I was sure this was really a suicide."

"It was," Tom said flatly.

"I know that. But I gotta ask. Is there anything that might come out later that's going to make me doubt myself?"

Tom sighed. He had been in similar situations himself and he knew that Anderson didn't deserve his indignation. He had been fair and professional from the start.

"No," Tom said. "It was exactly what it looked like. The bad part is there is going to be some bad stuff coming out about Joe. And I'm afraid a lot of it will be true. I guess he couldn't live with that."

Anderson thought for a moment and then said, "Yeah that sucks. Like I said, I feel like a shit for even asking."

Tom felt himself tearing up again. He shook Anderson's hand and said, "Don't worry about it."

He got out of the car and climbed into his own. He wiped his eyes, started the car and headed home.

CHAPTER 19

Tom found a space half a block from his apartment. He sat motionless in his car with the motor off for another twenty minutes. His head was pounding and it felt as though he had a great weight sitting on his chest.

After he made it upstairs to his apartment he headed to the kitchen and took the bottle of Jamison's that his cousin had given him for Christmas out of the cabinet and found a clean glass, then headed out to his tiny front porch. The cool night air helped him get most of his breath back and the whiskey helped flatten out his nerves. The street was quiet with the only sound coming from the sound of the sporadic traffic on Elmwood Avenue.

He lost track of time as his mind wandered over the events of the last two years. How had things gotten so fouled up? Finally at about four in the morning he went to bed.

A bell rang. Tom opened his eyes and the light seemed to penetrate his skull and hurt like hell. How much did he drink last night? The bell again, what was it? He looked at the clock on his nightstand. It was just past nine AM and somebody was at the door.

He went to grab his robe and realized he was still in his clothes from the night before. Was that a drop of blood on his sleeve? Two steps into the hall and he felt like throwing up. He took a few deep breaths and fought the urge as he got to the door.

It was Erica standing on the landing in her nurses uniform. Her dark hair was down and her hazel eyes were looking expectant. She looked at Tom and her eyes then betrayed a little bit of shock and then pity.

"Tom, are you okay?" she asked.

"So, you heard?" he responded as Erica came in and gave him a hug.

"Yeah. There were a couple of guys from B district in the ER last night and they were talking about an ex cop who shot himself. I didn't want to ask, but I had to be sure."

Tom pulled her close again. All the emotions of the previous night came back to him.

"I am so sorry," she said.

"So am I."

Erica took a step back and they just looked at each other for a moment. Finally she broke the silence. It had usually fallen to her to do so, especially towards the end of their living together.

"I had to see you and make sure you were alright," she said.

Tom just nodded.

She looked at him and sighed. "Do you want to talk

about it?"

Tom thought for a second. He didn't want to alienate Erica any further but he wanted to think things through before he said anything. He reached out and took her hand. "Not right now. I can't."

Erica looked down and then smiled slightly. "I didn't think you would."

"I will though. I just need a couple of days to process it. I can't tell you how much just seeing you at the door means to me."

Erica brightened slightly at that. "Will you call me and let me know about the wake?"

"Yeah," Tom said. "Maybe we could ride together."

"Okay," she said putting her other hand on his cheek. "Take care of yourself."

"Thank you, Erica." They embraced once more and she left.

Tom jumped in the shower and tried to wash the hangover off of himself with mixed results. He was slightly more awake, but his head still hurt. He made himself a bowl of oatmeal to try and line his stomach.

He thought about calling Lisa Walczak. Would she have gone home and into the room where her husband's blood was splattered on the wall and carpet? What would he say if he called anyway? Trying to convince himself to not feel guilty about it he decided to wait. He got dressed and grabbed his keys.

Before he got to the door Bob Stanley called to offer his sympathies about Joe. After that he got down to the real purpose of the call.

"Do you have a copy of the letter Joe wrote?" Stanley asked.

"No, I left it on the desk. I had a feeling I might be searched so I didn't want it to look like I had something to hide."

"Good," Stanley said. "Tom, I hate to ask this, but I'm starting a trial on Monday and I don't think we should put this off."

"Put what off?"

"I want to move for a dismissal of your part of the lawsuit."

"What?"

Stanley was unfazed. "I know you are probably in shock Tom, but with the letter and the some information I have from the DEA, I think we can move to have your name dropped from the suit."

"Jesus, Bob, isn't it a little soon?"

"I know it looks like the bloodthirsty soulless lawyer coming out in me," Stanley began. "But I may be tied up in court for weeks. I at least want to get this rolling before that happens."

Tom went silent. No, not yet. Joe's body wasn't even cold yet.

"Tom? Are you still there?"

"Yeah. I was just thinking."

"I have a contact with the Amherst PD and I can probably get a copy of the letter," Stanley told him. "I will tell Judge Meyers that his and Sheldon Sumner's are in the mail. At least let's take a shot."

"I don't know."

"Tom, listen, I am truly sorry about what happened to your partner, but you have to start thinking about yourself. You know this lawsuit is wrong and you have to be ready to fight it."

"I will be," Tom muttered.

Stanley went on, "The worst case scenario is the motion gets denied but we get to see if the plaintiff tips their hand to anything they come up with during their response. Tom, they sucker punched you and it's up to you if you want to fight back or not."

Stanley was starting to sound like he wasn't going to take no for an answer.

"Okay, go ahead," Tom finally said.

"Good. Where are you now?"

"I was just leaving for the office."

"Do you own a suit?" Stanley asked.

Tom had to think for a second. "Yeah, why?"

"Bring it with you. I was hoping you would agree to my idea, but I already put a call in to Judge Meyers' clerk. It's a long shot but I am hoping we can get in today."

"Today?"

"Like I said, Tom, I want to get this rolling. If this works like I hope it will at least it buys us some more time."

Stanley told Tom he would call him back with any news and they hung up. This was definitely a departure for Bob Stanley. In Tom's experiences with the attorney he never struck him as a gambler or the type to do something without looking at it from every possible angle. What could he do? He needed Stanley to help him navigate through the legal quagmire. He went back to his closet and grabbed the only suit he owned. It was dark blue and about four years old. It still looked like new due to the fact that Tom had only worn it a handful of times. He got a shirt and tie and dress shoes and put them into a garment bag.

Twenty minutes later he was at this desk at the agency. Grace looked surprised and said she hadn't expected to see him today. Thankfully Cal was meeting with a client, so he avoided having to rehash the suicide again. He had to clear his mind and focus on something. He took his notebook out and, starting at the beginning, reviewed everything he had written down about the Shields case. In all the commotion at Joe's house and the aftermath he really hadn't had time to think about his meeting with Donna and Katrina at the motel. Was Donna really safe? What if there was a copy or copies of the disc?

He went to Brian's office and had Brian help him with research on property titles to the farmhouse in Farnham, the club and anything they could find on Gary Shields, Mike

Manzella and Katrina Bedford. After a few hours of not finding anything new or incriminating they called it quits.

Tom's head had stopped throbbing, but now he was feeling antsy. He had to get out of the office. He drove over to the gym on Elmwood and worked out for forty-five minutes and then jumped on to the elliptical machine.

After his third mile his phone buzzed. He jumped off the machine and answered it.

"Tom, its Bob Stanley."

"What's up?"

"Judge Meyers will see us today at 4:30," Stanley said.

Tom looked up at the oversized wall clock. It was 3:15.

"I'll meet you at the courthouse."

"Good," Stanley said and clicked off.

At 4:25 a freshly showered and shaved Tom Donovan got of the elevator on the second floor of the courthouse just off Niagara Square. Most of the downtown parking garages were half empty at that time on a Friday which saved Tom from being late. He was still sweating bullets underneath his suit.

Bob Stanley stepped up to him as the elevator doors were closing behind him.

"I was getting worried you weren't going to make it until the clerk came out and said the Judge was running a little late," Stanley said.

Over Stanley's shoulder Tom caught the eye of George Frangos, attorney for the family of Derrick Trent, and he didn't look happy. Frangos appeared to be by himself.

Stanley guided Tom over to a wooden bench on the side of the corridor and sat him down. Tom noticed Stanley sat between himself and Frangos.

"Where is the rest of the mob?" Tom whispered.

Stanley frowned disapprovingly. "The mother won't be here, but I understand the Reverend Mason is on his way."

"Did he have to pick up the camera crew from channel seven?" Tom asked.

Stanley frowned again but didn't respond.

Tom looked down into a wastebasket next to the bench where someone had discarded a copy of the News. The paper was folded in quarters and it was upside down. Tom craned his neck to see one of the smaller headlines: *Lovejoy Area Woman Missing*.

The sub headline said: *Mother Suspects Foul Play*.

Tom looked into the basket. There were some discarded coffee cups on the bottom and what looked like a piece of gum stuck to the paper, but something about the headline gave him pause and he went to reach for it anyway.

Just then Judge Meyers' clerk came out and said they could come in.

After they were seated Stanley went into detail

about the new developments in the case and submitted a copy of Joe's confession to the judge. Frangos objected on the grounds that he hadn't had a chance to validate the authenticity of the letter. Further more, he said, it could be the case of one dirty cop covering for another one and then he just stopped short of saying that Tom might have coerced Joe into writing it.

Stanley responded that he had corroboration from a source inside the DEA that Joe Walczak alone was the one who had taken money from Derrick Trent and would subpoena Buffalo Police IAD to see if they had anything on Tom or Joe.

Frangos slipped up then and said he already had contacted internal affairs. When the judge asked him if they had anything incriminating Tom, he said they were still reviewing the information.

Judge Meyers leaned back in his chair and put the end of his pen up to his mouth. Finally he said, "What does it all mean Mr. Stanley?"

"Your honor," Stanley began. "I would like to have my clients name dropped from the plaintiff's lawsuit."

"What?" Frangos sputtered and almost came out of his seat.

The judge glared at Frangos. "Mr. Frangos please. I am as surprised as you are, but I would prefer if you used your inside voice in my chambers."

"I beg your pardon, your honor. But isn't the

defendant's council getting way ahead of himself?"

Stanley spoke up then, "Your honor, my client, a decorated police officer in this city for ten years had already testified about the death of Mr. Trent before a grand jury that chose not to indict. The unfortunate event cost him his career and his livelihood. Now after two years the plaintiff wants the last thing he has left, his reputation."

Frangos started to protest, but the judge shut him down. "Gentlemen it's after five o'clock," he began. "And I have had a pretty crappy week. This is not how I wanted to cap it off. Mr. Stanley there is no way I am going to order the lawsuit struck down with this short of notice."

Tom glanced at Stanley who was looking at the judge impassively.

"Furthermore," the judge continued. "I am more than a little disturbed at the apparent callousness that brought you here so quickly after the tragic incident last night." He looked at Tom who started sweating all over again. "No, I want to look this over. I will need until the end of next week."

"Thank you, Your Honor," Stanley said.

Frangos was still steaming. "Your honor, with all due respect I resent having to sit through this grandstand play by the defense's counsel. I certainly hope there won't be more of these theatrics moving forward." As he finished he glared at Stanley.

The judge stood up walked towards a coat rack.

He looked back at Frangos. "I don't give a crap what you resent at the moment Mr. Frangos. And as far as what you hope for, try this, if you move forward on this you better hope that you have insurmountable evidence regarding Mr. Donovan's involvement or you will be setting your client up for one hell of a counter-suit. We're done here gentleman."

As they left the judge's chambers Tom saw the Reverend Ezra Mason waiting outside. Mason took one look at Frangos' red face and knew the news wasn't good. Stanley guided Tom past them and towards the elevator. As they passed the bench they had sat on before Tom glanced down into the wastebasket only to see that it had been emptied. Mason was raising his voice behind him and started walking towards the elevator. The elevator bell rang and the doors started to open.

"Donovan!"

Tom turned around. Mason was ten feet away and it looked like Frangos was going to grab him if he got any closer. Tom just looked back. He felt Stanley's hand on his arm pulling him back into the elevator.

Mason held up a finger. "I hope you know this isn't over."

Tom stared back and said, "You know, Reverend, I knew the night it happened that it would never be over."

The elevator doors closed.

Chapter 20

Tom walked with Stanley back to the Ellicot Square building. Stanley looked both relieved and exhausted.

"I know you didn't want to do this Tom, but two good things came from it," he said.

Tom snapped out of his funk. "Such as?"

"Number one: I don't think Frangos got what he wanted from the Buffalo PD's Internal Affairs Division. And number two; I think they will think long and hard about the possibility of a counter suit."

"You know I wouldn't have the stomach for that," Tom said.

"Yes, I do. But they don't know that."

They walked in silence until they got to the buildings entrance. Stanley turned to Tom and said, "Again, I just want to say that I'm sorry you had to go through this so soon after the death of your friend. If anything you can forget about it for a week while we wait on the judge." He offered his hand to Tom and Tom shook it.

"Thanks, Bob."

"Now go mourn your friend. I'll be in touch."

Tom went back to the garage to get his car. He

realized he had left his notebook at the office so he drove back to get it. He found the notebook on the desk and was about to leave but something was nagging at him. He booted up his desktop and logged onto The Buffalo News web site. The headline he had seen at the courthouse was still on the home page.

Lovejoy Neighborhood Woman Missing.

Mother Suspects Foul Play.

The article said:

Buffalo Police yesterday found the abandoned car belonging to Rachel M. Eberle of the city's Lovejoy neighborhood in a field off Broadway. Ms. Eberle had been reported missing early Thursday morning by her mother, Helen Eberle of the same address, when she didn't return home from work. An initial police report stated that there were traces of blood on the vehicle's interior and Ms. Eberle's purse was still inside. A police spokesman refused to comment further on the ongoing investigation only to say that they had spoken to Ms. Eberle's ex boyfriend who witnesses verified was working a double shift on the night she disappeared.

When contacted by the News Mrs Eberle stated that she feared that her daughter may have been followed home from Showgirls Gentlemen's Club in Lackawana, where she worked as an exotic dancer.

"I always hated her working there," she said. "I was always afraid that something like this was going to

happen."

The News contacted the club's manager, who refused to give his name. The manager stated that while he hopes that no harm had come to Ms. Eberle, the clubs staff is vigilant in protecting the dancers from any kind of harassment. "The safety of our staff has always come first," he stated. "We are always on the look out for unruly patrons. Our parking lot is under video surveillance and the girls are escorted to their vehicles at the end of their shift." Calls to the club's owner Donna Shields had not been returned as of press time.

"Fuck me," Tom said out loud. He had half a mind to go home, grab his father's gun and take a ride over to the club. What would that solve? He turned off the computer, picked up his notebook and went home.

Tom felt drained and frustrated. Against his better judgment he grabbed a beer and went back out to the porch. He sat in the one lawn chair he owned and looked off into space. He took a few sips of the beer, but it disagreed with him so he set it down. After and indeterminate amount of time he felt his phone buzz in his pocket.

"Yes."

"Mr. Donovan?" It was Donna Shields. "Katrina and I have talked it over and we decided that we want to accept your offer."

Tom sat up. "What do you mean?"

"I arranged a meeting with Gary tomorrow morning

and we want you to be there, as a witness," she told him.

Tom thought for a moment and asked, "What do you want me to do?"

"Do you have a camera with a telephoto lens?"

"I can get one from the agency. Where are you meeting?"

"We went round and round about that," Donna began. "He wanted me to bring it to the club but I said no. Katrina said it should be somewhere in the open. We are meeting in front of the Central Terminal at 6:45 AM."

Tom thought about that. The shuttered Central Terminal was in the heart of the city's East side. It would be deserted at that hour, but it was one of the most heavily patrolled areas of the city.

"Listen, Donna, are you sure that this is a good idea?"

Donna exhaled and said, "I just want to look that bastard in the eye one last time and warn him if he causes any trouble for my sister I'll blow the lid off his whole sordid, disgusting business."

She sounded determined and sure of herself. Tom knew there was no stopping her.

"I take it you want me out of sight, taking pictures?"

"That's the idea," Donna said. "He agreed that he would come alone but I don't trust him."

A little late for that revelation, Tom thought. "I'll be there," he said.

"Okay. Goodnight." The line went dead.

Tom went inside and dumped the rest of the beer out. He stood by the sink and thought. The Shields matter may be coming to some kind of resolution but at a high cost. Rachel was missing and the threat of violence from Gary Shields and Mike Manzella was still a distinct possibility. His mind turned back to Joe and once again he thought of calling Lisa, but couldn't bring himself to do it. It was 8:30 and sleep was out of the question so he left and headed back to the agency.

Tom had a key to get into the front office door and his own door but what he needed was in a locked cabinet in Brian's office. Besides being the agency's resident computer expert, Brian was also in charge of maintaining all of the surveillance equipment.

Tom took the screwdriver he had brought from home and used it to jimmy Brian's door open. He turned on the light and walked over to the cabinet. The lock was integrated into the handle on the cabinet door. He fished around in his pocket until he found the lock pick he had taken off a fifteen year old kid a few years back when he was still on the job. He figured he would pick the cabinet lock and that way not have to explain the whole story about why he had forced his way into Brian's office.

After a few minutes he got the lock to turn and opened the cabinet. On the top shelf he found the bag containing the Canon digital camera with the telephoto lens. From the shelf below that he helped himself to a police scanner that could be plugged into his car's AC adaptor. He had used the camera a few times before and was comfortable with it. He needed one more thing. After rooting around the cabinet for a few minutes he found a small black canvas bag with a zipper on top. He opened the bag and took out the long-range amplified microphone. He had only seen it once before when Brian was playing with it. The microphone looked like a wand with a pistol butt attached. Also in the bag were the receiver and headphones. Brian had told Tom that the mike didn't get used too much because it violated all kinds of privacy statutes and that it was only for 'special occasions'. It doesn't get more special than this, Tom thought.

He shut the cabinet doors and put the pick in to turn the lock. When it didn't turn right away Tom put a little extra pressure on the pick and it snapped off in his hand.

"Shit!"

Part of the pick was just barely visible inside the lock. Tom doubted he could even pull it out with a pair of pliers, which he didn't have anyway. He put the mike back in the bag, zipped it shut, gathered up the other equipment and left.

He got home just after midnight and tested the microphone from his porch. It was pretty simple to use and Brian had told him it had a range of three hundred feet, but was susceptible to picking up background noise and the occasional unwanted radio signal.

Tom checked the camera's battery and then put everything away. He took a long hot shower and lay in bed for a while before giving up on the idea of sleep. He would just have to wait for sunrise.

Chapter 21

Tom was very familiar with the Central Terminal. Constructed in the late twenties, when Buffalo was on its way to becoming one of the major industrial centers of the Northeast, the terminal served as the Eastern terminus to the New York Central Railroad. Its seventeen-story structure could be seen from downtown all the way out to the suburbs. Shortly after the grand opening, though, came the Great Depression and rail travel diminished along with peoples disposable income. Things were pretty bleak for the railroad until the start of World War II. All matters of people and freight were shipped on trains and a second boom looked to be on the horizon. That too hit the wall after the war when America went car crazy. Railroads were merged and sold and the terminal languished until 1979 when Amtrak finally pulled the plug.

The massive structure fell into serious disrepair and ownership of the property changed hands several times. It had been cleaned out by self-described preservationists and looted by vandals. Heroic efforts had been taken to preserve and restore what was left, but it was an uphill struggle. Tom had spent about eight years of his life policing in the shadow of the Terminal. He had once chased a suspected mugger through the parking lot only to have the young man go over a fence and disappear. Another time he and his partner had been the first unit on the scene to check on the report of man lying on the ground near the front entrance. He arrived to find a homeless man he had previously seen panhandling on Broadway, frozen to death on the sidewalk. It turned out that the dead man was a decorated Vietnam veteran named Turner Jones who a VA doctor later described as "A textbook case on untreated PTSD."

The building itself gave off a strange vibe to Tom. Despite the broken windows and years of accumulated debris something about the building still seemed alive, almost like a hulking concrete ghost. He parked his car across Memorial Drive in a church parking lot and looked up at the building with the sun coming up behind it. It still gave him the willies.

The church parking lot afforded him the best vantage point of the Terminal without being conspicuous. He checked his watch, it was 5:45 AM. He checked for signs of life on the streets around him and saw none. He just had to wait now. He took the thermos of black coffee off the back seat and poured himself a cup. He plugged in the scanner and set the volume down to where it was barely audible. He checked the camera and the microphone and settled in.

At 6:42 AM a silver BMW drove past the church

lot right in front of Tom. He barely saw it in time before he ducked down. The BMW turned onto Paderewski Drive and parked on the right side of the entryway about twenty yards form the terminal. Tom looked through the camera. Part of the car was obscured by a small tree and the car was pointed away from his vantage point but he would bet any money that it was Gary Shields.

Less than a minute later a small blue sedan entered Paderewski. It must have come from the other side of Memorial because Tom had not seen it enter the traffic circle out front. The car drove in quickly did an abrupt U-turn and stopped facing the Beamer.

Tom turned on the microphone on and pointed it at the two cars with his left hand. He raised the camera back up with his right and saw Donna Shields in the blue sedan. Nothing happened for a moment and then the driver's side door of the BMW opened and out popped Gary Shields. He took a quick look around and then walked slowly over to the driver's side of the blue car. Tom couldn't see his face he could tell Shields was nervous by the tentative way he moved. He looked down and turned up the volume on the microphone. The headphones crackled and then became clear.

"Where's your dyke friend?" Gary said. Big mistake, Tom thought. Donna already looked pretty pissed off.

Never mind that," Donna snapped back. "I don't

have time for your bullshit. Do you want the notebook or not?"

"Sure, honey, but why all the drama?"

The police scanner crackled to life.

"I just wanted to remind you," Donna had started to say as Tom took the headphones off. He turned up the volume and heard the tail end of a transmission:

"... shots fired corner Broadway and Wick. All units respond."

Tom started to sweat. It didn't have the feel of a coincidence. As he looked up again, he saw Donna pass an envelope through the window to Gary. Just then a shadow flew by the camera. Tom dropped the camera to his lap just in time to see a newer looking black pickup truck turn on to the circle. The driver was wearing a tan baseball hat with silver hair showing out from underneath.

"Shit," Tom said. He looked quickly around the terminal grounds but Katrina was nowhere in sight. He reached under his seat for the .38.

The pickup accelerated and came to a screeching halt behind Donna's car. That had her boxed in. Gary bolted back to his car.

"Shit. Shit. Shit," Tom yelled. In his mind he knew he would never make it across Memorial Drive and the parking lot in time. He raised the camera and started snapping pictures.

A tall, stocky, middle-aged man emerged from

the pickup truck and started walking towards Donna, who seemed to be frozen. Tom zoomed the lens in and to his disbelief saw that it was Lieutenant Kruger, the Lackawana cop who had intervened the other night at the club. Had he followed Gary Shields? Had he arrived like the cavalry again?

No. He had a gun in his hand and was raising it up in and had it pointed towards Donna's car. What the hell? One more step and he would be point blank. Then a loud crack echoed across the parking lot and reverberated off the church's walls. Kruger's head snapped forward and then his body tumbled down to the pavement.

Gary and Donna sat motionless for a moment. Then Donna started screaming at Gary through the windshields of both cars. Suddenly Gary's back up lights came on and his car roared into reverse. He stepped on the gas and his tires spun. He almost lost control of the BMW turning it around toward the exit and then another loud crack and his rear window exploded.

Tom put all of the equipment down and started his car. It wouldn't be long before the cops figured that the call on Broadway and Wick was a false alarm and be down at the terminal in a hurry. As he pulled out of the church parking lot he saw Donna's car backing up towards the terminal and a small black-clad figure running towards it. Sure enough the scanner came to life again with a call out to the terminal.

Tom drove quickly down Memorial until he turned

left on to Fillmore and then dropped down to a more prudent speed. A few minutes late he was on I-190 headed downtown. He hoped that he had been far enough away from the fray that if there were any witnesses he hadn't drawn their attention. Over the scanner he heard the call go out for the watch commander. They must have identified Kruger and knew that this was no run of the mill Eastside shootout.

By the time he passed under the Peace Bridge he felt his pulse slowing down to normal. He exited on Niagara Street and had the sudden urge to park and clear his head. He crossed the drawbridge to Broderick Park and found a parking space away from the cars of the fisherman trying their luck off the walkway that ran about a mile South back under the bridge.

The first thing he did was peel off his jacket and notice that his shirt was soaked with sweat. He had been a little less that a football field away from the action and yet he felt like he had been right in the middle of it. He threw his jacket in to the car and then gathered up the surveillance equipment, bagged it and put it in his trunk.

He went around to the front of his car, sat on the hood and looked out at the Niagara River rushing by and Fort Erie, Ontario on the other side. The sun had risen all the way up and there wasn't a cloud in the sky.

He thought about Kruger and realized he wasn't protecting Tom the other night but rather protecting the club.

He must have been on Manzella's payroll. Who better to look out for your dirty business than a Lieutenant in the local police force. After Joe's revelation the other night nothing like that would surprise him. He still wondered what would tempt a man like Kruger to do Manzella's dirty work. Had he been slighted in some way? Was he facing an impending retirement and thought he deserved more than living out his life on a public servant's pension? Only Kruger could possibly know the answer to that, and he wasn't going to be telling anyone his side of the story anytime soon.

It was over. After today Tom couldn't imagine Donna and Katrina hanging around town anymore. They had proved, in no uncertain terms, that they were willing to back up their promise of reprisal. As long as Donna had Katrina on her side she had proved that she was not one to be pushed around.

He thought about Rachel Eberle, the dancer. She had been somebody's daughter. She had been somebody's mother. He would have to add her to the list of people he would always feel responsible for hurting in one way or another. She had vanished and was probably dead. He had put her in harms way but Manzella and Shields had given her the final push. Guys like Manzella and Shields would always be around manipulating the weak and the naive to carry out their twisted schemes.

Tom felt a chill on his damp shirt now from the cool morning air. It was just after 8:00AM. He pulled out his phone and dialed.

"Donovan's," Bonnie said.

"Bonnie, it's Tom."

"Hi Tommy. Are you looking for Hugh?"

"No, actually I was wondering if Whitey was around."

"Yeah he's in the back. Hold on, sweetie, I'll get him."

CHAPTER 22

Tom's alarm went off at 2:00 AM. He had slept soundly for five hours. One thing his father had encouraged Tom to do when he started to box was to force yourself to take a nap before a fight. "It clears the mind and relaxes the muscles," his dad had said. Tom got dressed, grabbed a couple of things and went downstairs to wait.

Fifteen minutes later Whitey Brennan's Cadillac pulled up in front of the house. There was already someone in the passenger seat so Tom jumped in the back and found himself sitting next to Whitey's son Pete.

"Evening Tom," Pete said.

"Pete."

The man in the front passenger seat turned around. It was Pete's older brother Dan.

"Tommy, how ya doing?" Dan asked.

"I'm doing okay. It's been a pretty crappy week though. How's the concrete business?"

Dan gave a slight smile and said, "The weather's been very agreeable. We've got work lined up until the beginning of July already." Dan looked to his brother for confirmation.

"Could be our best year yet," Pete said.

Eight years earlier Tom's grandfather, Hugh, had staked the Brennan brothers seed money to start a concrete business. They had started out small with a few driveways but had since moved on to larger commercial jobs. Like their father they both stood over six foot three but each one carried a little more muscle that the old man.

From the drivers seat Whitey turned around and looked at Tom.

"Are you ready, Tom?"

"Yeah, let's go."

Chapter 23

It was 3:45 AM. The car did a second pass in front of the club pulled around the corner onto a side street and parked.

"Seems pretty quiet," one of the men in the car said.

"There's no time like the present," the driver said.

The four men exited the car and walked quickly to the club's front entrance.

Marty the cashier was straightening the bills in the cash drawer, getting ready count it out at closing. The outer door opened and a man with a revolver and a ski mask came in. Right on his heels came three more men, all larger than the first man. Two of them had sawed off shot guns and the other one had a handgun. Marty's hand instinctively reached for the trouble alarm on the side of the counter, but before he could reach it one of the larger men reached across and grabbed Marty by the hair on the back of his head. Marty let out a grunt and then the man slammed Marty's head down on the cash register.

Larry the doorman, still with two black eyes from his broken nose, opened the door from the bar into the foyer and was immediately struck in the temple with the side of a gun. He stumbled back into the bar. Three of the masked men rushed in past the spot where he landed.

There was no one on stage and no music. There were a few customers left at the bar and a few of the girls who appeared to be having a drink before heading home. Frank the manager was at the end of the bar where he had been talking to the barmaid. A big guy who bore a resemblance to Larry the doorman was standing next to him. Everyone was frozen where they stood except for the masked men who were fanning out across the bar.

"What the fuck?" the guy who looked like Larry said.

"Shut up and don't move," said the taller guy with the handgun.

The fourth gunman came in to the bar practically carrying Marty by his hair. Blood was running down Marty's face from a gash on his forehead. One of the girls screamed.

Frank, in a moment of outright fear or bravado, took that moment to turn and bolt for the stairs to the office. He huffed his way up the stairs, thinking that he heard footsteps behind him. He made it into the office and started to push the door shut when the smaller gunman threw his shoulder into the door. The force of the man putting all his weight into the door knocked it back into Frank's face and sent him reeling backwards onto the floor. The masked man rushed in and kicked Frank in the ribs. Frank let out a howl and looked up into the barrel of a gun.

"Get up," the masked man said.

Frank stood up as sweat beaded on his forehead

"Sit down," the man said still pointing the gun in Frank's face.

Frank backed up and bumped into one of the wooden chairs in front of his desk. He finally he worked up the urge to speak. "You're making a big mistake," he said.

"Shut it!" the masked man yelled. He swung his free hand and punched Frank in the stomach doubling him over. "That's for being a mouthy prick." Then he hit Frank on top of the head with the butt of the gun. Frank collapsed into the chair. "And that's for being a shitty boss."

When Frank opened his eyes after the blow he saw that one of the other, larger men had come into the office and moved out of sight behind the chair he had been deposited into. The man in front of him slapped his face.

"Where's Manzella?" he asked

Frank was a little dazed. "He's not here," was all he could say. It earned him another slap.

"I can see that dip-shit. Where is he?"

"God damn it, I don't know," Frank blurted. "He left about an hour ago."

The second gunman had taken two large zip ties out and was using one to secure Frank's hand to the arm of the chair. He pulled it tight.

"Ow! Fuck! Take it easy," Frank whined.

His other wrist was bound and the smaller man was back in his face.

"Okay, fat boy, I believe you. We'll catch up with Mikey later. We want something else anyway."

"I don't have anything," Frank pleaded.

"Where do you keep the shit?"

"What are you taking about?" Frank asked, pathetic.

"The oxy and the coke and whatever else you're peddling."

Frank shook his head and said, "You're crazy."

The larger masked man stepped up to the side of the chair and brought the butt of the shotgun down onto the back of Frank's hand and then stepped back. Frank screamed a few more obscenities and his eyes filled up.

"That's strike one," said the man in front of him. "We know you're selling shit out of this dump so just tell us where it is."

"You got it wrong man. We-" Frank began, but was not allowed to finish.

The man came from behind Frank again but this time on the other side and brought the shotgun down on that hand. More cursing and now actual tears streaming down Frank's face.

"That's strike two," the man in front of him said and he cocked the hammer on his gun and pressed the barrel into Frank's knee. "I'm ahead in the count Frankie and I got all night."

"Behind that bookcase," Frank said through gritted teeth.

"What?"

"That's a false wall behind the bookcase," Frank said and he nodded in the direction of the shelving unit off to the side. The man in front of Frank nodded and the other man went and pulled it down violently sending the contents spilling across the floor. Sure enough there was a trap door about three feet tall and three feet wide cut into the drywall.

The man pulled the panel off and tossed it aside. He bent over and peered inside then let out a low whistle. "Kinda dark in there but it looks like a lot of stuff," he said.

"Good," said the man in front of Frank. "Oh, one more thing Frankie."

Frank looked whipped. He looked up at the man with glassy eyes and said, "What?"

"What happened to Candy?"

Frank shook is head. "I don't know," he whispered. "They said it was the ex-boyfriend-"

"Bullshit! Pick up a newspaper. He had an alibi." The gun was back in Frank's face.

From next to the trap door the larger man said, "He looks like too much of a pussy to do the girl himself."

The man in front of Frank said, "True, but I bet he knows who did it and as long as he isn't going to tell me I can just pretend it was him and I'll have to live with that." He cocked the pistol again.

"Jesus! It was Manzella!" Frank blurted out. "He did it, alright?" He shook his head to try to get the sweat out of his eyes. "I warned her before about her big mouth. I told her he was crazy and not to mess with him. But the stupid whore wouldn't listen!"

The smaller man in front of Frank un-cocked the gun and put it into his left hand. Then he made a fist with his right hand pulled it back and hit Frank in the eye sending Frank and the chair over on their side.

The smaller man said to his companion, "Grab the surveillance machine."

From the floor in front of the desk Frank heard the sound of cables being wrenched out of their sockets. He heard footsteps and then looked at the backs of the two men leaving.

"Motherfucker! I know who you are!" he yelled.

The two men turned around and looked back. Then the larger of the two men set the video machine down on a chair and walked back to stand over Frank. He pulled a large hunting knife off his belt and bent over Frank. He used the point to lift Frank's chin up so he could look into his eye.

"Listen boy," he whispered. "I don't know what you think you know, but it would be best to forget it." He bent a little lower and hissed, "Because if I hear about you speculating about tonight and making wild accusations, I will personally come back and gut you like a deer on opening day."

All the fight seemed to leave Frank's body and the two men left.

Their two companions were waiting at the bottom of the stairs. One of the men who came out of the office asked, "Everybody locked in the cooler?"

"Yeah."

The smallest member of the party was looking up at the ceiling and when he found what he was looking for he went behind the bar and grabbed a small metal garbage can. He packed it down and topped it off with as many paper bar napkins as he could find. He scanned the bar and found a bottle of 100 proof rum and poured half of it into the garbage can. He jumped up on the bar and removed a cigarette lighter from his pocket and lit the can. He was holding the can as close to the smoke detector as he could. Just as the can was beginning to get too hot to hold the alarm went off and the strobe lights over the exits lit up. He set the can down on the bar and jumped off.

The four men barged through an emergency exit causing another alarm to go off and disappeared into the night.

Chapter 24

Tom arrived at the office shortly after noon on Monday. He had spent the previous day sleeping and sitting around his apartment with his phone turned off. He had turned it on briefly when he finally broke down and called Joe Walczak's widow, Lisa.

Lisa was putting on a brave front. She thanked Tom for calling and said that he had been a good friend to Joe, before and after the shooting. She told Tom that she realized that Joe's problems were mostly of his own making. They spoke for about twenty minutes and then she said she had to pick up Tyler from her mother's. Despite Lisa's assurances Tom still felt a pain gnawing at his stomach.

Grace was on the phone when Tom entered the reception area on Monday. She looked up and made eye contact and gave a little wave. Behind her desk Cal's door was closed. Tom went down to his office. Sherry's desk looked like she had been there working on something, but she was nowhere in sight. Tom moved to his chair and saw that someone had left a copy of the Buffalo News on his desk. He read the headline on the paper's front page.

Drugs Found After False Fire Alarm.

Early Sunday morning the Lackawanna Fire Department was called out at 4:10 AM to respond to an alarm at the Showgirls Gentleman's Club on Dona St. The call-out took a bizarre turn when firefighters entered the building and found what at first appeared to have been and armed robbery. Lackawanna police, who were also on the scene, found several employees, two who had been assaulted, and several patrons locked in the walk-in cooler in the bar's kitchen. The club's manager was found in his office bound to a chair and beaten. During their inspection of the building officials reportedly found a storage space off the office containing a large amount of meth-amphetamine, cocaine and prescription pain killers, the value of which has yet to be determined.

A spokesman for the Lackawanna Police said that witnesses indicated that just before the bar was about to close four masked men rushed in the front entrance and forced them into the cooler. Less is known about what happened to the club's manager, Frank M. Cambrio, as of press time, he was refusing to cooperate with the police.

Calls to the home of the club's owners Gary and Donna Shields of Buffalo were referred to their attorney, Miles Brewer, who released this statement: "Mr. and Mrs. Shields were shocked and saddened to find out that some of their employees may have been dealing drugs out of Showgirls. They had believed that the management team they had put in place was as determined as the to keep that type element of out of the bar. Sadly they were mistaken."

The police spokesman also went on to say that given the amount of drugs recovered the club may have been part of a larger narcotics operation, and were seeking assistance from the DEA.

Only one arrest warrant has been issued so far. Authorities are looking for Michael P. Manzella, a parolee previously convicted on narcotics charges, who has been spotted in the club numerous times.

Story continued of page A6

Tom folded up the paper and placed it in the wastebasket next to his desk. He took out a blank expense report and filled out the top. He sat back in his chair and stared at the document for a few moments then realized he had no interest in filling it out. The expense report went into the trash also.

Tom went down the hall and knocked on Brian Dinkle's partially open door. Brian was staring intently into the large monitor on his desk. Tom wasn't sure if Brian had heard him so he stepped inside and was about to say something when Brian spoke first.

"Dude, you need to get a better set of lock picks," Brian said with out looking up.

"Yeah, sorry about that. I was in a little bit of a hurry."

Brian finally looked up from his work. "Well, don't

worry. I already fixed the lock on the storage cabinet and I told Grace that I had to jimmy my office door open when I locked my keys inside after hours."

Tom smiled. "Thanks Brian. I owe you."

"That you do, Tommy boy."

Brian started to turn back to his computer and thought of something. "Oh, was there anything on the camera you needed saved?"

Tom shook his head. "Nope, never had a chance to use it."

He walked down the hall and stood in front of Grace's desk. She looked up and smiled at him. "Are you alright, Tom?" she asked.

"Yeah, I'm fine Grace. Pretty rough week but I'll be fine. Is Cal in?"

"Yes, he is. Go on in."

Tom tapped on the door and opened it. Calvert Frederickson was seated by his window blowing cigar smoke outside. He looked at Tom and motioned towards a chair. Tom sat down.

"Dirty habit I know," Cal said looking at the cigar.

"Why don't you quit?" Tom asked.

Cal gazed at Tom and said, "It's hard to break old habits." And let that sink in for a second. "I remember when I started in '78 one of my first calls was for a body stuffed in a crawl space on the West side, man it was ripe. This old homicide dick shows up and the first thing he does is light a cheap assed cigar. 'Kills the smell,' he says. And he gives me one. Now by the time I got in to the Homicide squad in '94 you wouldn't even think of lighting a cigar near a crime scene. But then sometimes the smell of a stiff would linger with you." He paused and took a protracted drag, then exhaled. "I guess you could call it a 'coping mechanism.'"

They sat silently for a moment. Tom wasn't sure what, if anything, Cal was getting at.

"I take it you saw the paper?" Cal said finally.

"The one you left on my desk? Yeah, I did."

One corner of Cal's mouth turned up. "When I was with the police one thing they told us we could not abide vigilantes. The problem with folks taking justice into their own hands is sometimes they can get carried away."

"I could see where that would be a concern," Tom said. "But I think that the staff of Showgirls probably got off easy."

Cal nodded and looked out his window. "Who's to say? Too bad about Manzella slipping away though."

"Uh huh. And what about Shields?" Tom asked.

"All I know is what I read in the paper," Cal answered and blew smoke out the window. "His lawyer claims that Shields's only crime was trusting the wrong people. Oh, and he had no idea a convicted felon was selling drugs out of his night club."

"Yeah, I'm sure."

Cal set his cigar down and looked at something on his desk. "Mr. Shields attorney called this morning and said that his client will not be paying anything else to us since we never did really find his wife."

Tom shook his head. "Sorry about that."

Cal looked at him and said, "I know it's not from lack of effort on your part. And the first check for five thousand already has cleared so I told him he could kiss my ass if he thought he was getting that back."

Cal went quiet again and was just looking at Tom as if he were trying to figure out how to put something into words. Finally he said, "The more I found out about Shields and Manzella the more I was glad I gave this to you Tom. I don't know if anybody else would have gotten this close to the truth."

Tom didn't know what to say, so he just gave a nod. Cal stood up, a sign for Tom to stand up too.

"Isn't Joe's wake today?" Cal asked closing his window.

"Yeah, the visitation is at four and seven."

"You need company?"

Tom was a little surprised by the offer but then remembered they had all worn the uniform at one time. "No, thanks though. Erica is picking me up."

"Oh," Cal said raising an eyebrow.

Tom allowed himself a slight smile. "We're still friends."

"Oh, didn't mean anything."

Tom turned toward the door. Cal had returned his chair back behind the desk.

"Pretty strange about Lt. Kruger though, huh?" Cal said before Tom opened the door.

Tom stopped and looked back. "How so?"

"I was talking to a friend downtown. No one has any idea what he was doing at the Central Terminal on a Saturday morning. He told his wife he was going fishing," Cal said as he shuffled some papers on his desk. "You throw in the bogus 911 call as a possible diversion, no witnesses, no shell casings. It must be some kind of wild story that nobody seems to want to tell. It's a shame to see a fellow officer go down like that."

"Yeah, it's a shame alright," Tom said as he opened the door and left.

Chapter 25

It was a warm sunny mid-morning three days later when Captain Samuel Dipietro got the call. He was just pulling into the parking lot of the Amherst Audubon golf course when his phone went off. After a hurried apology to the rest of his foursome he rushed home and put on his uniform.

Forty-five minutes later he pulled up in front of the house on Nottingham Terrace. The large brick homes on Nottingham had been built on the grounds of the Pan American Exposition in the Twenties and Thirties by the upper class that had been created during Buffalo's economic rise and were still home to some of the cities wealthier residents.

As he pulled up he saw that the crime scene and medical examiners vehicles were already there. Captain Dipietro signed in with the patrolman at the foot of the driveway and went under the yellow crime scene tape.

A group of officers was gathered towards the rear of the house. When Sam reached them he saw Detective Michaels coming out of the back door.

"Andrea."

"Cap."

"Who called it in?"

Michaels flipped open a notebook she was carrying and said, "The attorney, Miles Brewer, called this morning and said that he was supposed to meet with Shields at Ten O'clock to discuss the strip club and Mr. Shields never showed. He tried to call him on his home number, his cell and at his office. Brewer met Yancey and Phillips here and discovered the back door was open but no Shields. Yancey looked into the garage door there and saw Shield's BMW inside with the drivers side door open, so with Mr. Brewers blessing he broke the window with his baton and found Shields next to the car."

"Any word on the wife?" Dipietro asked.

"No sign of her, Cap. The back door of the house was open and the alarm silenced. I took a quick look around and it looks like the house was searched"

"Somebody tossed it?

Michaels frowned. "Not exactly tossed. Just searched like who ever did it knew what they were looking for."

Dipietro turned to the garage. "You been in there?"

Michaels shook her head and said, "No, Yancey didn't get a pulse and the body was cold so we called Homicide. We started a canvas but none of the neighbors seem to be home right now"

Dipietro nodded. "Okay, take a couple people in

the house and see if you can find anything of interest, then let the techs go in and see if there are any prints." He turned and walked towards the garage.

Just then a grey haired man in a suit walked out of the side door of the garage, one of the homicide detectives. Dipietro recognized him immediately.

"Hey, Chuck."

"Hey, Sam. Didn't think I'd see you here."

"The chief called," Dipietro told him. "Said this might get a lot of attention so it was all hands on deck." He pointed back through the door. "So it's definitely Shields in there?"

"Yeah. He still had his wallet and ID on him. Looks like he has been there at least twenty four hours but we'll have a better idea after the medical examiner is through."

"How did it happen?" Dipietro asked.

The detective peeled off his vinyl gloves and tossed them into a trashcan. "Well, at first blush it looks like the shooter popped him when he was getting out of his car. The body was lying face down on the driver's side. We were getting ready to roll him then we noticed something when one of the tech's camera flash went off."

"What was that?"

"Two marks on the side of his head just below the hairline."

"Like a stun gun?" The Captain asked.

"Probably," Chuck answered. "And then we saw

marks on his wrists that looked like they'd been made before he was killed. Looks like he had been restrained."

Depietro thought for a moment and then said, "You heard about the mess at his club the other night? You think it was the people supplying Manzella come looking for a pound of flesh."

Now it was Chuck's turn to think. He finally shook his head. "Could be, but it doesn't quite fit. Those people are animals if they're who we think they are. He wasn't tortured and when he was killed it was quick. They outfit that these guys were tangled up with would have either used this to send a message or get rid of him completely."

"Okay then, if it wasn't the cartel, then who would go through the trouble of tying him up before they waste him?" He looked back at the garage as the overhead door opened.

"Could be somebody wanted to ask him something and he either gave it up or he didn't," Chuck said. "Either way he had outlived his usefulness."

The coroner's attendants were making their way up the driveway with a gurney.

"What about the wife?" Dipietro asked. "Any sign of her?"

"From what I understand, she's been missing for a few days."

Sam thought about his nephew and his involvement with the Shields. Tom had told him his business with

Shields was finished when he had seen him at his sister Rose's house on Tuesday. No, Tom couldn't have possibly had anything to do with this, could he? He was a hothead and could be impulsive, but he was no killer.

"Captain," Detective Michaels called out as she approached from the back door of the house.

"Anything?"

"There's a safe in the basement, underneath an old workbench. Judging by the dust that was displaced in front of it it looks like it's been opened recently."

"Could have been Shields," Dipietro said.

"Or who ever tased him and tied him up," Chuck offered. "The shooter gets the combination from Shields, doesn't get what they want and pops Shields."

"Or gets what they want and pops Shields anyway," Michaels said.

Sam took a moment to ponder all of it. While he was still thinking Michaels continued, "And we may not necessarily be looking for a he."

Now both men looked at her.

"There's a partial footprint in some sawdust in the workshop. It is a little small to be a man's."

"Mrs. Sheilds?" Dipietro asked.

"I'm not sure. It looks like a boot-print. Something similar to what I wore when I was in uniform. I just can't picture Mrs. Shields running around her Nottingham Terrace estate in combat boots."

"Are they getting pictures?" Dipietro asked.

"Yeah, we cleared out and let the forensic team go in," Michaels answered.

"I sure would like to talk to the wife," Chuck said. "Provided she is still alive."

"I have it on fairly reliable authority she is," Dipietro offered. "I'd also like to talk to her, but I have the feeling she may not want to be found."

The two detectives just looked at him as if they were waiting for him to go on. Right then Sam Dipietro decided that he would keep what he knew to himself, for the time being. He would reach out to Tom first and find out if he knew anything about the matter.

Down the street he could see the news trucks starting to arrive. Nothing to tell them yet. So far all he had was more questions than answers. He sighed to himself and thought that this was probably going to be a long weekend.

Made in the USA
Middletown, DE
14 November 2019

78672301R00156